RED SHADOW

PAUL
DOWSWELL

BLOOMSBURY

LONDON NEW DELHI NEW YORK SYDNEY

Bloomsbury Publishing, London, New Delhi, New York and Sydney

First published in Great Britain in May 2014 by Bloomsbury Publishing Plc
50 Bedford Square, London WC1B 3DP

www.bloomsbury.com

Lines from Molotov's speech quoted on p.104, translated by Rodric Braithwaite,
Moscow 1941: A City and Its People at War © 2007 published by Profile Books

Lines from *Three Sisters* by Anton Chekhov © 1998 published by
Bristol Classical Press

A CIP catalogue record for this book is available from the British Library

ISBN 978 1 4088 2624 9

MIX
Paper from
responsible sources
FSC® C020471
www.fsc.org

Typeset by Hewer Text UK Ltd, Edinburgh
Printed in Great Britain by CPI Group (UK) Ltd, Croydon CR0 4YY

1 3 5 7 9 10 8 6 4 2

To John,
Wish you were here,
and also to Mary, George, Grace and Hannah

Moscow
October 1940

Misha looked at the grey clouds and shivered. That afternoon it was cold enough for a thin layer of ice to appear on the puddles on Moscow's pavements. He was pleased, he supposed, at this first sign of very cold weather because it meant an end to the *Rasputitsa* – the season of soggy rain and mud that preceded the winter and summer.

When he crossed the great bridge over the Moskva River to the Kremlin, the wind buffeted him and he wrapped his coat tightly around his slim frame. His half-hour walk home from school was nearly over.

Five minutes later he reached his family's apartment inside the Kremlin.

'Mama, I'm back,' he shouted as he entered the hall.

There was no reply. Anna Petrov was always home before him.

He knew something was wrong as soon as he entered the living room. A tray with a china tea set lay scattered

1

on the floor, spilt milk and tea leaving dark stains on the Persian rug among the shattered fragments of porcelain.

Misha called out again, panic in his voice. 'Mama! Are you all right?'

Perhaps she was unwell and sleeping? He went at once to his parents' room. It was exactly as his mama had left it that morning. He looked in the other rooms. All were empty. Maybe she had been taken to hospital?

He started when he heard the door open. 'Mama?' he called out. 'What's happened?'

It was his papa. Yegor Petrov was a sickly colour, sweat glistening on his forehead. 'She has been taken, Mikhail,' he said, before he crumpled and tears ran down his face.

Misha had never seen his father cry. He stood there feeling useless, reeling at the terrible news, not knowing what to do. 'Let me make you some coffee, Papa,' he said.

Misha sat at the dining-room table waiting for his papa to collect himself, watching his hands trembling as he lifted a cup of coffee to his mouth. Eventually Papa said, 'Colonel Volodin summoned me to his office at five o'clock. Mama has been arrested by the NKVD. She has been declared an enemy of the people.'

Within a week they discovered she had been sent to a camp in the east for ten years, with no 'right of correspondence.' Misha was filled with despair. For several days he could not bear to go to school. Who had ordered such a thing? What reason could they have to take his mother away?

A month after it happened Misha pleaded with his papa to talk again to Colonel Volodin, to try to find out more. His father said the Colonel had disappeared too. In a frightened whisper he told Misha they thought he had been liquidated, and that they should never speak of Mama again.

CHAPTER 1

May 1941

Mikhail Petrov was in the bathroom washing his hair in the basin when there was a brisk tap at the door. He recognised the knock at once. *RAP bap-BAP.* It could only be Valentina Golovkin, come to walk with him to the afternoon shift at School 107. He hastily slipped on a shirt and rushed to let her in, towel-drying his hair as he hurried down the corridor of the apartment.

She gave him a smile when he opened the door. 'Good afternoon, Misha. Like the haircut. Very stylish,' she said, smirking at his dishevelled appearance. Misha thought maybe it was time to visit the barber but he liked his hair long and floppy at the top.

'I won't be long, Valya,' he said. 'Come in and wait a minute.'

'Don't forget we have to pick up the Princess,' she said. 'And she always slows us down so hurry with the hair-drying!'

The Spasskaya Tower clock began to chime the opening notes of the communist anthem 'The Internationale', as it did every quarter-hour, and Valya shouted out, 'We're going to be late!'

A couple of days a week they went to collect Galina Zhiglov to drop her off at a local primary school on the way to their school. Valya said Galina reminded her of that Russian fairy tale about a *tsarevna* – a princess – who never smiled.

Galina lived in an apartment barely a minute down the corridor from Misha's. Her father, Kapitan Zhiglov, gave him the creeps. He knew that his mama and papa had been friendly with him once, but the friendship had ended quite abruptly. Misha sometimes wondered if the Kapitan had anything to do with his mother's arrest.

There was no Mrs Zhiglov. The rumour Misha had heard touched on divorce and a relationship with the head of the Central Museum of Soviet Exports. The Kapitan had been given custody of Galina, which was a mystery to all who knew him. Zhiglov was NKVD. The Soviet secret police were not known for their nurturing qualities.

When they reached the Zhiglovs' apartment, Valya knocked and they waited. An anxious young woman peered around the crack in the door. It was Lydia,

Zhiglov's maid. She looked relieved when she saw who it was and opened the door wide.

'Galina, your friends are here for you,' she called. She turned to Valya and Misha and gave them a look of weary exasperation. Lydia, they knew, spent most of her time trying to entertain Galina. Zhiglov himself worked long hours at the Lubyanka, the headquarters of the NKVD. They said he was a close adviser to the head of the secret police – Lavrentiy Beria. Misha had seen Beria around the Kremlin too – a stubby bald man with spectacles. He could have been a provincial tax inspector but for the palpable air of menace that surrounded him, almost like a cloud of cologne.

A solemn little girl emerged from the shadows and gave them both a formal nod. She was dressed beautifully in a calico floral-print dress and had her golden hair tied in two neat plaits. A red and gold enamel Young Octobrist badge on her collar caught in the light.

'And how are you today, young lady?' said Valya.

'I am very well, thank you. And how are you?' she answered with unnerving poise.

Lydia dashed out with a coat, hat, gloves and scarf, and Galina stood like a mannequin as the maid draped these clothes around her.

Misha resented having to walk Galina to her school.

Valya was the only person he felt he could talk to honestly and he couldn't do that when the little girl was there.

Valya was the only one among his school comrades who knew his mother had been arrested. When it happened, he had trusted her enough to tell her. But even with Valya he didn't usually talk about his mother. Recently he was beginning to wonder if others had found out too. Maybe their parents had connections with the NKVD and someone had let it slip. These days he always felt a twisty anxiety when he went to school. Children of 'enemies of the people' could expect to be denounced and humiliated in front of their classmates, then barred from further education. It had been seven months now since his mama's disappearance and, as yet, it had not happened to him.

He was even more surprised that he and Papa still lived in their Kremlin apartment. In the weeks after Mama's arrest he woke with a start every time he heard noises in the night, expecting them both to be dragged away. But that had not happened either. Misha thought that maybe it was because his father was one of Stalin's secretaries. They had a friendship of sorts.

Valya, Galina and Misha emerged from the grand apartments of the Arsenal building into bright sunshine.

Misha loved the spring – didn't everyone in Moscow? That early May afternoon, as they began their walk to School 107, it was so hot they even took off their hats and carried their coats.

The authorities had introduced two shifts in schools to cope with Moscow's swelling population. Misha liked being on the second shift – 2.30 until 8.00 – with the morning free for homework and chores. It meant he could have a lie-in. And Papa usually worked very late so he sometimes got to see him before bedtime, if Comrade Stalin finished his meetings early.

Just as they were about to leave the Kremlin grounds Misha spotted a familiar face. When the family had first moved to the Kremlin, he had been introduced to General Rokossovsky in their apartment. The General had been briefing his father on naval deployment along the sea frontier with Japan, so Yegor Petrov could prepare a report for the *Vozhd* – the Boss.

Rokossovsky had a gallant manner and it was whispered he had been a cavalry officer for the Tsar before the Revolution. Papa had told Misha he spoke to everyone, from the *Vozhd* to the cleaning ladies, with the same courtesy, which made him one of the most widely liked men in the Kremlin. Misha liked him because the General had always smiled at him when he saw him in the corridor, whereas most of the adults he passed ignored him completely. But not long after Misha met him he vanished – along with many other senior army officers. Everyone thought he had been liquidated. Yet here he was again, very much alive.

Misha went over to speak to him. 'Comrade General, how nice to see you again. How are you?'

Rokossovsky smiled pleasantly and looked him straight in the eye. 'I am well, young citizen,' he replied. 'I have been resting.' Then he gave Valya and Galina a brisk little bow. Misha introduced them and Rokossovsky said to Valya, 'Ah yes, I know your father.'

As he spoke, he brushed a stray hair from his eyes, and Misha noticed all the fingernails on his hand had been removed. It was all he could do not to flinch. 'Comrade General, if I may say so, I am pleased to see you back,' Misha muttered, his heart racing. What could he say to Galina if she asked about his fingers? Could he pretend he hadn't noticed?

As they walked away, Valya turned to Galina with a smile and asked, 'So, what have you been doing this morning? Have you been keeping Lydia busy?'

Valya always knew what to say to Galina, and Misha was relieved when the little girl answered with her usual composure.

'Lydia told me about the house spirit Domovoj when she was reading me bedtime stories,' said Galina. 'He lives behind the stove in the kitchen and he comes out at night to pinch naughty girls who are rude and ungrateful.'

'And has he pinched you?' asked Misha, trying to keep a smile from his face.

'Certainly not. I am neither rude nor ungrateful,' Galina said indignantly. 'But I have found out more about Domovoj in one of Papa's encyclopedias. He gets angry if a house is not cleaned properly. So I told Lydia to polish every surface so there is not a speck of dust.'

Misha smiled to himself. Lydia had been outwitted. Galina was going to grow up to be the kind of girl that terrified him.

Once they had dropped her off at her school, Misha said, 'Did you see his hand?' Valya nodded. She looked as shocked as he was.

At that point they emerged on to a main street making further discussion of the subject too dangerous. Thousands of people jostled along the pavements, like cattle being herded into pens. There were streams and counterstreams, like cross-currents at a river confluence. It was an odd experience. Misha was sure Moscow hadn't always been this crowded. But every year it seemed that more

11

and more people flooded in from the countryside to find work here and a roof over their heads. New factories were being opened all the time and the city was alive with the whirr of machine tools and the tang of white-hot metal. There was a constant, sticky, acrid smell of hot tar too. Everywhere you went they were digging up roads, laying drains or cables.

The streets in central Moscow at most times of the day were almost as bad as travelling by tram, but at least you were outdoors, away from the concentrated smell of humanity. Misha was struck by how shabby most people in the street looked. After four years living in the Kremlin, he had grown used to the finely tailored suits of the political elite and the cashmere silk and pearls of their wives. Most people outside the Kremlin bought clothes second- or third-hand on the market. And no one ever seemed to smile. The newspapers said no one smiled in capitalist countries. In contrast the workers and peasants of the Soviet Union who appeared in the newsreels were bright and full of enthusiasm for their lives and the advances of the Revolution. Misha was beginning to real-ise not everything he read was to be taken at face value.

A hundred metres ahead there was a sudden screech-ing of brakes and a piercing scream which cut through the afternoon chaos. In the distance they could see a lorry reversed halfway out of a side road. Pedestrians continued to hurry by.

As they got nearer, they saw that a boy was lying sprawled on the pavement. Only the lorry driver was kneeling beside him, trying to revive him. No one wanted to get involved. Getting involved meant talking to the Militia – the Moscow police. Talking to them laid you open to all sorts of awkward questions.

Valya grabbed Misha by the arm. 'We must help.' They arrived, slightly out of breath. The old driver looked terrified.

'The poor child,' he said. Then he started to admonish the unconscious boy, half in anger, half in anguish. 'Why didn't you look where you were going, you silly boy? What are they going to tell your mother?'

The boy's left leg was sticking out at an odd angle, but more worrying were the flecks of blood around his mouth.

'Don't move him,' said Valya. 'We need to wait for an ambulance. He may have broken his back.'

A harsh voice startled them all. 'You, girl, did you see what happened?' Two Militia men had arrived.

'No, comrade. We have just got here.'

'Then what is your business here, citizens?' said the taller of the two officers. He sounded more reasonable.

'We are just trying to help,' said Misha.

'You shut your mouth,' said the smaller Militia man. 'My comrade was talking to the girl.'

The driver spoke up. 'I was reversing into the side street here, and the boy just walked into the road.'

'You two,' said the shorter one to Misha and Valya. 'Passes.'

They fumbled through layers of clothes and produced their identity papers.

The taller officer stepped forward and took them. He nodded and said, 'All is in order, citizens. Be on your way.'

Out of earshot, Misha mumbled, 'No wonder people don't like to stop and help if that's all the thanks they get.'

The afternoon had started unhappily. He wondered if it would get worse.

CHAPTER 2

The incident had shaken them both and for a while they walked in silence.

They passed a large billboard, plastered on the side of a building, showing the hero pilot Shura Kuvshinova in her flying helmet and heavy overalls. Her perfect teeth were gleaming white and she was advertising toothpaste.

Seeking to lighten the mood, Valya nudged him. 'That reminds me, I have an exam today. Wish me luck.'

'Aeronautics?' guessed Misha. She had told him about this before.

Valya was good at maths and science. She could work out algebra and trigonometry in her head, and she knew exactly what she wanted to do when she'd finished school. Like Shura Kuvshinova, Valya wanted to be a pilot and she already spent most Rest Days at the Pioneer Young Pilots Club in Vnukovo, taking enthralled young boys and girls on glider flights.

'I need to pass this for Moscow University, Misha. I need a high mark too – there's a lot of people who want to get on that course. And no matter what Comrade Stalin and the other Politburo comrades say about the equality of women, you still need to be better than the boys to be taken seriously.'

'But what a waste of your life. You're such a good cook,' teased Misha. 'And so handy with a needle and thread.'

'Misha, *you* are a block of wood.' She tapped his head. 'And in here is hollow!'

Ten minutes later they said goodbye at the gates of School 107 and Misha took a deep breath and headed for his classroom. Today was going to be a chore. Day Two in the school week always was – trigonometry, evolutionary theory, chemistry. Misha was not much of a scientist, although he tried as hard as he could. His real interest lay in plays and novels: Chekhov, Tolstoy and, most of all, Shakespeare. He liked words and what they did to your imagination. He was good at writing too, so much so that his classmates said he should edit *The Pioneer*, School 107's newspaper. He was flattered and said he could be persuaded. But he was beginning to regret that. Barikada Kozlov was the current editor, and he would be a powerful enemy to make. Barikada's father worked for the

NKVD, just like Galina's father, Kapitan Zhiglov. Misha wondered if they knew each other, but he was shrewd enough not to ask. A question like that could get you denounced as a spy. Sometimes he wondered if Barikada had found out about his mama. The boy looked at him occasionally with a knowing smirk.

And besides, *The Pioneer*'s monthly diet of the school's sporting achievements, the necessity of 'world revolution' and the perils of 'anti-Soviet conversations' didn't really appeal to Misha. He had already realised it would be dangerous to produce a more interesting magazine.

As Misha walked into his first-floor classroom, he was greeted by a hail of catcalls from Sergey and Nikolay, who had been watching through the window as he and Valya arrived. 'A bit out of your league, isn't she, Mikhail?'

'Has she let you kiss her yet?'

'Get lost!' said Misha, but he could feel himself beginning to blush.

Yelena was there too, sitting by the window, her blonde bob glowing in the spring sunshine.

She gave him a broad smile when he came to sit next to her, and whispered, 'They couldn't get a girl to look at them if they were the last two boys in Moscow!'

'She's just a friend,' he said, feeling a bit flustered. 'We just live near each other.' She looked surprised and for a second Misha thought he saw a flash of relief in her eyes.

She was working on an embroidery of Lenin for the school sewing circle. She had told him about it before in rather more detail than he wanted to hear – a series of vignettes showing the life of the leader of the Revolution from his birth in 1870 to his death in 1924.

'A fine likeness, Yelena,' he said, looking at the embroidery. 'You've got his steely gaze just right.'

She blushed now, and wondered if he was teasing her, which he was.

They talked a little about the volunteer teaching they both did as part of their *Komsomol* duties. Like any ambitious Soviet youths, they were both in the *Komsomol* – the communist youth group for aspiring Party members. Yelena had recently begun to give reading classes to peasant children just arrived in Moscow. She was shocked to discover many were completely illiterate.

And every Day One Misha also went out before school to teach literature to workers in their lunch break, over at the Stalin Automobile Plant. He was so good at it the students had asked him to do an early evening class as well. School had agreed to that – letting him go two hours early every Day Four. Teaching was definitely the career for him, and he loved the enthusiasm of the workers he taught. He could see a genuine interest in their faces, quite unlike the obligatory displays of zeal required for political speeches and parades. Recently Stalin's daughter Svetlana had even sought him out at the Kremlin to help her with her literature homework. Misha kept quiet about that though. A good *Komsomol* cadet did not boast. Only his father and Valya knew.

Yelena said, 'Will you be going to the meeting this breaktime? It would be nice to walk there with you.'

'I was thinking of going,' said Misha, as if a member of the *Komsomol* could do anything else. 'Remind me what it's about.'

'It's Barikada again. The need to unmask class enemies.' She dropped her voice to a whisper. 'I don't like him but I do think he gives the comrades a good moral lead.'

Misha liked Yelena but she irritated him too. She was too eager to please, always spouting the Party line straight from *Pravda*. They all believed in the Soviet cause, but Yelena spoke of her duty as a communist with a religious reverence that made Misha uncomfortable. She had given a breaktime talk last month on 'Comrade Stalin – the greatest genius of all times and all people', which had made Misha's toes curl with embarrassment. But that was the problem with living in the Kremlin. He'd seen Stalin in the flesh. His greying hair, pockmarked face and terrifying piercing stare were quite different from the friendly figure they read about in the magazines.

Misha's afternoon chemistry class was interminable and he even began to look forward to the break at 6.00, and Barikada's speech. He walked over to the canteen with Yelena and they sat down on the sill of a large window. His friend Nikolay came over to join them.

He and Nikolay had known each other since they were ten and Nikolay had been one of the few friends who hadn't greeted his move to the Kremlin with sour envy.

Barikada's subject was one that Misha was wearily familiar with – 'class enemies', such as landlords, priests and nobles, who 'lurked' in factories and schools, hiding under false proletarian identities. Such 'former people', Barikada assured them, were intent on sabotaging the achievements of the Revolution and betraying the country to foreign enemies.

Misha's attention began to drift until he heard his name and anxiety twisted his guts. He realised everyone was looking at him. 'And what I have to tell you, comrades, is that *Komsomol* cadet Mikhail Petrov was seen last Rest Day emerging from a church.'

There were audible gasps around the room but Misha relaxed a little. This was serious but it wasn't about his mother. He felt Yelena's hand on his arm.

'Comrade Kozlov,' he said indignantly, 'can you substantiate this accusation?'

Misha wasn't going to deny it but he would like to find out who had denounced him.

'Comrade Petrov, you must know that a good communist would never reveal the name of the citizen who has done his duty to the Party in reporting this serious misdemeanour.'

Misha shook his head. Before he could speak Barikada said, 'I have spoken about this matter to the school Komsorg, and propose that Comrade Petrov be immediately deprived of his *Komsomol* membership.'

A murmur of discontent went around the room.

This was much more serious. The Komsorg was a sour young official with a tough peasant face, named Leonid Gribkov. Misha guessed he was about thirty. He oversaw the activities of all *Komsomol* members in the school. Misha disliked him as much as he disliked Barikada; they were two of a kind. He wondered how much Gribkov knew about his family.

With these two ranged against him, he knew he needed a convincing defence.

'Comrades, you all know I have no respect for religion. Only last month I wrote a piece for *The Pioneer* in support of the Union of the Godless. But my

21

grandmother, like many older people, is still in thrall to the backward practices and beliefs of the old regime. As she can barely walk on her own, I went there to take her home.'

The class cheered and Misha realised with relief that their discontent was directed at Barikada, not him. He felt his confidence growing. 'Surely, comrades, we can show humanity towards those unlucky enough to be born before the Revolution, and who have not had the benefit of a sound, scientific education.'

Barikada shot Misha an angry look. 'I recognise the democratic will of the school comrades, and the reasoning of Comrade Petrov, and withdraw my demand,' he said.

The incident had taken the wind from Barikada's sails. He made one or two more comments about the need for vigilance against class traitors and saboteurs, and then sat down to lukewarm applause.

Misha felt uneasy. He had won this particular battle but what would happen next? Barikada was blushing red with humiliation.

As they drifted out of the canteen, Yelena leaned closer as she walked beside him. 'He's frightened of you,' she whispered. 'He thinks you're after his position as editor of *The Pioneer*.'

'He's welcome to it,' said Misha, trying to laugh off this very public attack. If this was all because his friends had suggested he be the editor of *The Pioneer*, he was definitely not interested. He felt slightly sick and held on tightly to his books and papers in case his shaky hands dropped them.

She placed a hand on his arm. 'Don't worry about him, Misha. He can't hurt you – no one likes him.'

Misha nodded, although he wasn't reassured by what she had said. One of the lessons he had learned was that, in the Soviet Union, being liked was not important. Wielding power was important. Being feared was important. And so was knowing the right people. Barikada certainly knew that too, which was why Misha often saw him huddled together in whispered conversation with the Komsorg. Whenever Misha tried to talk to Leonid Gribkov, he had blanked him or answered with single-word responses.

Misha needed some fresh air. They walked out into the school courtyard and Yelena said, 'I'm going with friends to see *A Girl With Character* on Rest Day. Would you like to join us?'

Misha wasn't in the mood for a musical about a zealous young activist exposing the corrupt director of a state grain farm. Besides, he had a good excuse. He had already arranged to see Dynamo Moscow play Spartak Moscow with his friends Nikolay and Sergey.

When classes finished, there was still some warmth in the pleasant spring evening. He was pleased to see Valya waiting for him at the school gate. 'Isn't it nice to walk home in daylight?' she said.

Then, sensing he wasn't his usual self, she said, 'What's up, Misha?'

He told her about what Barikada had done and his concerns about the Komsorg. 'Gribkov's always had his beady eye on me. He's never liked me.'

Valya had a theory about the Komsorg. 'Leonid Gribkov is an engineer, Misha. Actually, from what I hear, a failed engineer. He thinks everyone should be designing crankshafts for tractors and ailerons for aeroplanes. I'm sure he thinks your literature specialism is more than a little bourgeois! That's what this is about.'

When Misha first started school, good manners, correct grammar, going to the theatre were all seen as being bourgeois – the habits and affectations of the former ruling classes. They left you open to attack as an enemy of the people. But things had changed over the last ten years. He was sure that Comrade Stalin and the other Politburo heads valued people who brought culture

24

to the workers. Ballet, theatre, literature – they were a central part of being a 'cultured' communist. You read about that every day in the youth magazines they had in the school library.

'I'm not bothered about his stupid prejudices,' said Misha.

Valya put a hand on his shoulder. 'Be careful. A word from Gribkov could get you into a lot of trouble.'

Misha was keen to change the subject. 'How was the exam?'

'It was OK,' she replied. 'I think I did most of it right. Pretty simple really, as long as you know the difference between velocity and speed.'

Misha nodded sagely. He didn't, but he wasn't going to let her know.

'We're lucky, aren't we?' she said. 'Papa says it was chaos just after the Revolution, when they abolished exams and homework. I'm so glad we go to school now, not ten or fifteen years ago.'

'I'm glad we do everything now,' said Misha. 'It's amazing what we've achieved in twenty years.'

'Listen to us,' laughed Valya. 'We sound like *Pravda*.'

Misha laughed too. 'We'll be singing "Life Is Getting Better" next,' he said and began to hum the tune. When he was younger, they sang it in the Pioneers as they sat round the campfire. Life was simpler then. Life was always simpler when you didn't think about things or question them. At that moment, he wished he was eleven or twelve again, chanting 'Thank you, Comrade Stalin, for our happy childhoods' with his classmates at the end of the school day. Back then, he didn't have to worry about snakes like Barikada and Gribkov denouncing him, and he believed Comrade Stalin was the Greatest Man on Earth. And Mama was still there to greet him when he came home from school.

Just before they reached the great bridge over to the Kremlin, Valya said she had to drop in on a friend who lived close by and would see him tomorrow. As they said goodbye, Misha remembered something he had been meaning to ask her.

'Hey, Valya, there's a banquet tomorrow night – one for the Ministry of Foreign Affairs in the Grand Kremlin Palace. It's going to be huge. All the Politburo will be there, Foreign Minister Molotov, of course, and Beria. The head waiter said he needs all the waiting staff he can get and did I know anyone . . . so I thought I'd ask you.'

Valya's eyes opened wide in surprise, but she wasn't as excited as Misha expected she would be.

'They pay twenty roubles a night,' he said.

She shrugged. 'They say Beria's a lecherous creep,' she

said. 'I've done this kind of thing before. You have to wear a tight little waitress's uniform and the men get drunk and leer at you.'

Misha thought of the stout middle-aged Politburo chiefs and shuddered. He felt grateful he didn't have to put up with that sort of thing.

'I'm sure you can steer clear of Beria. There'll be hundreds of people there.'

'I've always wanted to see the inside of the Grand Kremlin Palace,' Valya said, 'and twenty roubles sounds all right for a few hours' work, so I'll do it.'

Misha remembered the excitement he had felt at his first banquet in the summer of 1939, just before the war broke out in Europe. That one was a very grand affair for the German Foreign Minister, Herr von Ribbentrop, in honour of the treaty of friendship the two countries had just signed.

He remained puzzled about the treaty to this day. Until the week before it was signed, the Soviet people had been told that the Nazis were the greatest enemy of the Revolution in Europe and that communists in Germany were cruelly persecuted. Yet now the two countries were friends. But, as Mama and Papa had both told him, sometimes it was best just to go along with things and not ask any awkward questions.

Getting that first waiting job was pure luck. One of the waiters had been taken ill. Misha was asked to take his place. It wasn't a difficult job. There would be no carrying of plates of soup or heavy dishes. He just had to stand at the back of the banqueting hall and offer any assistance needed. They found him a waiter's outfit that fitted, and being a tall boy, even then at fourteen, Misha managed to look the part.

Herr von Ribbentrop appeared ill at ease, he remembered, yet smiled throughout the whole event. Misha had read that enemies of Nazi Germany referred to him as a 'champagne salesman' and he certainly had the look of a man whose life's work consisted of pampering the rich and greedy.

There were scores of toasts drunk to the mutual health of Hitler and Stalin, and the continued success and prosperity of both countries. Some were drunk with sweet Crimean champagne but most with vodka. Misha had occasionally drunk his father's vodka, sometimes at family occasions, and a few times when his father was out. Just a couple of shots made him feel a bit dizzy and giggly, so he was amazed when the diplomats and politicians knocked back gallons of the stuff. Towards the end of the evening, he was called on to deliver a fresh supply to the *Vozhd* himself. Misha went to the kitchen and was handed an open bottle of Beluga vodka, one of the finest brands produced in the Soviet Union. Curious to try this delicacy, he nipped into a side corridor, where he was certain that no one could see him, and took a minute sip. It tasted of nothing whatsoever and was such a shock to his palate he almost spat it out. What he was delivering to Stalin was plain water.

CHAPTER 3

Dusk was falling as Misha crossed the great bridge over the Moskva. He stopped and stood a while looking at the Kremlin. A couple of years ago he had felt a real sense of pride when he looked at this view. That feeling vanished the day Mama disappeared. Now these elaborate buildings looked sinister to him.

Maybe that was why he was drawn to Valya, he thought. She had lost her mother too, although hers had died in childbirth, along with a baby boy, when she was fourteen; and her father, Anatoly, worked on Stalin's secretarial staff, like his own father. These things gave them a special bond. What a shame she was two years older than him.

He walked through grand palaces and apartments to the Cathedral Square, dwarfed by four great churches, each topped with their own golden spheres. As a child, he always thought the spheres looked like gigantic onions and he still thought that now. The whole Kremlin complex was like a fairytale palace.

As the last glimpses of light disappeared over the horizon, spots of rain fell on his face. Misha hurried past the 'Little Corner' of the Senate building, where Comrade Stalin had his offices and apartment. He was nearly home.

First, though, he had one final chore to do. He had to ask Galina's father if he needed him to take her to school the following afternoon.

Kapitan Zhiglov answered the door. He was still wearing his green NKVD cap and the familiar uniform of breeches and black boots. Misha noticed bruises on his knuckles and shuddered a little, wondering what he had been doing that day at work. Despite his sinister uniform, Zhiglov looked a bit like a film star. He had sleek, black hair, which he combed back across the top of his head, and a little toothbrush moustache. Valya had told Misha she thought he was very attractive and Misha never lost an opportunity to remind her that he probably combed his hair back to hide a bald spot, and that his moustache was exactly the same as Hitler's. Misha wondered if she'd told him that she fancied Zhiglov to put him off her. She could probably tell he had a hopeless crush on her.

'Ah, young Petrov,' said the Kapitan. 'And where is your friend Valentina?'

31

'She has gone to see a friend, Kapitan,' said Misha. He felt as though he was talking to his *Komsomol* commander.

Zhiglov held his gaze for a few moments longer than necessary, which made Misha begin to sweat a little, then he smiled. It was an unsettling gesture which, despite the Kapitan's white even teeth, made Misha think of a crocodile.

'I have come to ask if you would like me to collect Galina tomorrow,' said Misha. Sometimes the child had other activities on Day Three.

'I would,' said Zhiglov. 'I will instruct Lydia to ensure she is ready for you.' He gave a brief nod, then closed the door with a gentle click.

A short walk down a grey stone and marble corridor on the second floor took Misha to the Petrovs' imposing wooden door. He turned the key in the lock and entered the empty apartment. Papa would probably not be home until midnight. Comrade Stalin worked into the early hours and quite often kept the secretarial staff at their desks until two or three in the morning. Misha thought no one else worked as hard as his father. Work completely dominated Yegor Petrov's life. He was like those people in Chekhov's *Three Sisters* 'who don't even notice whether it's summer or winter'.

Once, all five members of his family had lived in this sumptuous apartment. Mama and Papa and his elder brother and sister, Viktor and Elena. They were twenty-six and twenty-one now, and had both gone to the western republics – Viktor to Kiev and Elena to Odessa. His mother's absence left an ache like a poorly tooth, but Misha didn't usually mind being on his own. He and Papa got along all right most of the time.

He thought again how much he would like to live somewhere else. Yet when they had first arrived at the apartment, Misha couldn't believe his good fortune. One week they were living in a squalid *kommunalka* workers' apartment, sharing a cooker with four other families, and having to wash once a week at the local public baths, the next he was inside the Kremlin. They had even been given a little holiday home – a *dacha* – out to the south-west of Moscow. Papa had been lucky. He knew the right people. He had served with Comrade Stalin in the Civil War. They had fought together.

Misha dimly remembered a story from early childhood about his papa saving Comrade Stalin during the siege of Tsaritsyn. An assassin, one of the Tsar's former officers, had tried to shoot him as the Bolshevik high command planned their defence of the town. Yegor Petrov had knocked the weapon from the man's hand. The battle that followed had made Stalin's reputation and Tsaritsyn had been renamed Stalingrad.

In early 1937 *Pravda* had run an article on the teachers striving to eradicate illiteracy among the thousands of peasant families who were arriving in Moscow every month. A photo of Yegor was there on the front page with two of his students. That must have been what caught Stalin's eye. As soon as he discovered his old comrade was living in Moscow, he sent a message asking if he would come to live and work at the Kremlin.

But Stalin was very unpredictable. People around him would disappear for reasons no one could fathom, while others remained, their lives hanging by a thread. Misha had heard they called them 'the walking dead'. Maybe he and Papa were among them.

Perhaps his mama's disappearance was the start of it. A test of loyalty.

What other reason could there be for her arrest? Anna Petrov had come from a poor village in Belarus. She had been starving until the Revolution, as she often reminded Misha when he was little and refused to eat his dinner. She had educated herself in one of the new schools the Soviets had founded, becoming one of the first of her village to be able to read and write. Papa had often been busy with work, and Misha and his brother and sister had all been inspired and nurtured by their mother. Look at his elder brother, Viktor. Despite being in school at a time when exams and homework had both been abolished, he had gone on to work on the construction of the Magnitogorsk Steel Works – the biggest in the world, as the newsreels often boasted.

His mama had been an exemplary communist – forever volunteering, as he did now, to teach literacy in the evening, after her job as an elementary school teacher during the day. It made no sense to Misha that she should be declared an enemy of the people.

His train of thought was broken by the sound of a key in the lock.

'Hello, Papa. You're home early,' he said.

Yegor smiled and looked relaxed. 'The *Vozhd* went early to his *dacha*,' he said. 'There'd been a row with some of the high-ups. I could hear them through the office door. Some intelligence report from England came in, about the Nazis invading the Soviet Union in the spring. It's preposterous. Why would they do something so stupid? The *Vozhd* told me afterwards he thought the British were trying to scare him into an alliance. "Churchill needs all the help he can get," he said, "and it's not coming from me. The imperialist powers can tear themselves to pieces all by themselves."'

Misha thought about telling his papa what Barikada had said and asking whether he could stop taking Grandma to church. But his father looked so happy he didn't have the heart to spoil the moment.

CHAPTER 4

Misha woke the day after the banquet for the Ministry of Foreign Affairs feeling sluggish. It had been a very late night. Twenty courses of caviars, borsch soup, chicken, beef, lamb, sturgeon, salmon, stewed and fresh fruit, all washed down with champagne and either spiced or pepper vodka.

Valya had been there too, slightly to Misha's surprise, and he watched her handle the unwanted attention of the guests with her usual elan, but she looked even more exhausted than him when they had finished.

After a hurried breakfast, he put on his *Komsomol* uniform. He was required to wear it when he went to give his talks to the Stalin Automobile Plant workers.

He looked in the mirror and felt safe. Everyone recognised the red scarf and the Sam Browne belt and knew that whoever was wearing it was a young man or woman with a great deal of promise. Only the best were allowed to join the *Komsomol*, when they reached sixteen. That was how you got to be a member of the Communist Party – something every ambitious school boy or girl needed to be. And maybe, Misha thought, it would count in his favour if anyone else denounced him? Maybe it would make a difference if they were trying to decide whether to shoot him or send him to a prison camp.

He left school early to go to the automobile plant and was delighted to see at least twenty workers had come along to his class. Word seemed to be spreading. Today he introduced his students to Shakespeare's *Richard II*. They listened to what he had to say and seemed to appreciate the points he made about the play. When the class finished, some of the workers insisted Misha join them in a bar close to the factory. He didn't really want to go but didn't want them to think him aloof either. He was worried that alcohol might make him less cautious about what he was saying with other people around to judge him, maybe even betray him.

It started to rain heavily just as they got to the bar, which was in a little courtyard off the main street of the proletarian district, with plush red seats and stools and small wood and iron tables. That early in the evening it was half empty but it soon filled up with bedraggled customers seeking shelter from the weather.

One of the students – Misha thought his name was Vladlen – insisted on buying him a drink. Misha liked the fellow – well, he was barely more than a boy. He was quick to answer questions in class but always made sure the others had a chance to answer and that he didn't dominate the group. He was an assistant foreman too, a bright young man with a future. Like Misha.

In the corner of the bar there was a small coal fire which cast a lovely warm glow. As he reached the end of his beer, Misha began to relax enough to accept another when Vladlen insisted on buying him one.

The bar was now full to bursting and the noise was deafening, especially with the gramophone in the corner playing the jazz soundtrack from *The Jolly Fellows*. His drinking companions started to tell jokes.

Vladlen told one about a Frenchman, an American and a Russian, all stranded on a desert island. '"One of them catches a fish, but it's a magic talking fish and it offers them three wishes if they will throw it back."

"'I'll have a million dollars and I want to go back home," says the American. "I'll have three beautiful women and I want to go back home," says the Frenchman. The Russian is left all alone. He says, "I'll have a crate of vodka. And as we were all getting on so well, I want the other two to come back.""

They all laughed at that, although Misha had heard it before.

Vladlen seemed pleased at the success of his joke. Misha noticed he was drinking faster than the rest of them, and litre glasses too. Vladen leaned forward and waved his hands for them to huddle together and listen.

'Can you keep a secret?' he said. The others all nodded their heads. 'Three men in a prison camp,' he said, as quietly as the noise in the bar would allow. 'The first one says, "I am here because I supported Yezhov."'

Misha blanched. He couldn't believe Vladlen was telling a joke about Beria's predecessor as head of the NKVD, who had now disappeared. He looked at the others. They had fallen silent. Their stony faces giving nothing away. Vladlen didn't notice and blundered on.

'The second one says, "I am here because I opposed Yezhov." Then the third one says, "I am Yezhov!"'

Vladlen burst out laughing but only then did he notice no one else was joining in. He deflated like a balloon. 'What's wrong with you all?' he muttered.

Shortly after, he stormed off into the night.

Everyone seemed quite subdued after that. It had spoiled the evening and the cosy bar now seemed stifling. Misha was glad to step out into the cool night air, fresh after the rain. As he walked through the damp streets to the nearest metro stop, he remembered that his mama and papa never drank carelessly. They prided themselves on being cultured people. Even when they had all shared the single-room *kommunalka*, they had made sure Misha and his brother and sister all had their own towel and toothbrush. They all wore underwear and ate with knives and forks.

Thinking about the *kommunalka*, Misha made an impulsive decision. His old home was here in the proletarian district, a few minutes' walk away.

Within five minutes he had reached the outside of the building and was gazing up at the light coming from their old apartment. Misha's family had lived in part of the dining room. Once, finely dressed ladies and gentlemen had eaten there. By the time the Petrovs arrived, four separate families were crammed into the same space. The first thing they were shown when they moved in was a strict timetable, showing exactly when each family was entitled to use the bathroom and kitchen. The walls that separated their allotted dwelling places were thin enough to hear the slightest cough from the family next door, not to mention the arguments.

He looked around and memories of playing Reds and Whites out in the street came flooding back. None of the children wanted to be the Whites – the class traitors and reactionary elements in the Civil War. Inspired by the *kommunalka* rota, his brother Viktor had suggested a 'class traitor rota' to the children so they could take it in turns.

As Misha stood in the street, the door opened and someone came out. Misha let the woman leave, then tried the door. It never did close properly and he pushed it open now and stood in the hallway. The smell of the place was still exactly the same. That overpowering mixture of antiseptic, cold cabbage and stale frying, that clung to your clothes all day. All of a sudden he was ten years old again.

As he stood in the hall, he remembered other things, things long suppressed. They had known a family upstairs. The father was not a friendly man. Occasionally they would hear terrible rows between him and his wife. Once, they heard her shouting, 'If only you had kept your mouth shut, we would still be living in Kharkov.'

They knew something serious had happened when the usual morning stomping about and shouting were entirely absent. No one came home for lunch either. Someone always came home for lunch.

That evening Misha crept upstairs with Elena, and on the door was an official-looking document, stamped with the seal of the NKVD, instructing no one to enter the apartment nor remove the paper from the door. Even back then, Misha had heard of the NKVD. They were like the bogeyman in a fairy tale. But this was the first time he had seen something that told him they really existed.

Worse was to come. Two weeks later, Misha was alone in the apartment one evening and there was more shouting on the stairs. He went to look. Two men, dressed in drab green uniforms with breeches and black leather boots, were dragging a terrified man down the corridor. Another uniformed man came down the stairs carrying a small child under each arm. The man pushed past, nearly knocking Misha over, and one of the children looked at him desperately. Misha could still picture her now, tears streaking her face. The men hissed at him to get out of their sight. He fled with the smell of polished leather and stale sweat in his nostrils.

Afterwards, in the apartment, he felt totally alone. Usually the building was full of noise, but that evening the only sound he heard was footsteps on the floorboards. Nobody in the *kommunalka* was in the mood for talking.

Now, on that spring evening there in the hallway, Misha felt a tightening in his chest as he realised the NKVD had infected every part of his life.

The rain started again. He wrapped his coat tightly around himself and hurried to the metro.

CHAPTER 5

When Misha got back to the apartment, he remembered Papa had asked him to tidy up before he went to bed. As he searched for somewhere to put a pile of magazines that was taking over the living-room table, he opened a cupboard in the hallway they rarely used.

That cupboard was full of junk from his childhood. He smiled when he noticed a board game called Workers and Capitalists – a Soviet version of Snakes and Ladders with Revolutionary Guards and top-hatted bosses. There was a chess set too, with the figures modelled as Bolsheviks and counter-revolutionaries. His father had been very proud of that. It had been a gift from the Chairman of the Supreme Soviet. Misha wondered who got to play as the counter-revolutionaries, and whether or not it mattered if they won a particular game. Were you meant to play to lose if you were the counter-revolutionaries? Misha had half forgotten about that chess set, because it had disappeared shortly after Mama was taken away.

His eye caught something else glinting in the darkness of the cupboard. It was a box of Fry's chocolate biscuits, empty except for the wrappers, which they couldn't bring themselves to throw away. Mama had brought it home one day – one of many exotic delicacies she had discovered at the *Insnab* foreign provisions shop for Western workers in Moscow, which the families of the Party high-ups were also allowed to visit.

Soviet packaging was so plain and grey and Misha and his brother and sister had never seen anything quite so lovely. Each biscuit in the box was beautifully wrapped in gold or silver foil, or crinkly red or green cellophane. It was a whole day before anyone could bear to open and eat one. After that they didn't stop – gorging themselves on this delicious, smooth chocolate and buttery, crumbly biscuits in a single evening.

Seeing these chocolate wrappers reminded him of how Mama and Papa had both taken to life in the Kremlin with surprising ease.

He remembered how, when they started to be invited to Kremlin banquets, Mama had sometimes worn her hair down – she had beautiful, thick, curly locks, cut just above her shoulder, like Valya's – and occasionally she would even wear an elegant green evening gown. Comrade Stalin himself had taken quite an interest in her, she had hinted in her breakfast conversations. Misha remembered that with some unease. Even at that age he could see how she had enjoyed the attention and how uncomfortable Papa looked when she talked about it.

Then there were the friends they made. All at once the apartment seemed to be full of glamorous people, like the Usatovs. He was a naval attaché at the Kremlin, a very charming man from Leningrad, who had travelled all over the world and regaled them with tales of the splendours of New York and Tokyo and Paris. He had a beautiful younger wife. Mama had loved her company. She often came round for coffee and they would laugh all the time as they talked. Under the couple's influence Mama and Papa began to enjoy the best French wines and would look down their noses at the 'sweet stuff' from Rostov or Stavropol.

But then people they knew inside the Kremlin began to disappear in the middle of the night. It wasn't just the workers and the peasants from the *kommunalkas* who disappeared in the Great Purges. Being at the heart of power didn't protect you at all.

Out of the blue, Mama and Papa stopped buying expensive food and Mama went back to wearing her peasant dresses and headscarf. All of a sudden they no longer seemed so carefree. The dinner parties his parents hosted became more serious affairs, without the riotous laughter that had kept Misha awake until the early hours. Then Mama was taken away.

There were a few things he remembered which he hadn't been able to make any sense of. Just before Mama disappeared, his parents had had a terrible row. He had heard them both shouting. They had made up by the morning, but he still wondered what they had fallen out about. And just after Mama disappeared he had found an envelope in a cupboard stuffed with thousands of roubles. He knew it must have had something to do with his mama's disappearance, but he could never imagine what, and he hadn't dared mention it to Papa.

CHAPTER 6

The following Day Four, when he returned to the Stalin Automobile Plant for his early evening class, Misha's study group was missing a member. Although he felt that familiar knot of fear in his stomach, he could not say he was surprised. In the Soviet Union retribution was often swift and Misha had expected there might be trouble in store for Vladlen. *He* would never have said anything to the authorities. But there were always others who would. Maybe Vladlen had an apartment worth nabbing? Maybe someone coveted his position as supervisor at the plant? Now he was gone. Misha looked over the group of workers and wondered if it was worth asking where he was – just in case he had the flu or something like that. But his courage deserted him. He tried not to think of what might be happening to Vladlen and moved on to the text they were studying. 'Here we are: *Richard II*. Act three, scene two.'

The class seemed rather flat that evening and Misha was glad when it ended. As he was gathering his notes to leave, the Political Organiser of the factory came into the room. Misha had seen him before. A dumpy figure in an ill-fitting suit with a pasty white face, he reminded Misha of the Komsorg back at school. Leonid Gribkov would probably look like that in twenty years' time.

The man did not introduce himself; perhaps he felt the Communist Party badge on his lapel was all he needed to establish his authority. 'Citizen, I have heard good reports from the comrades in your class.' He paused. 'But I also hear you are a known associate of the anti-Soviet saboteur Vladlen Melnikov.'

Misha could feel his legs weakening. All of a sudden he felt sick.

'Comrade, I spoke only once with Citizen Melnikov, in the company of other comrades after a class.' Misha felt a mixture of indignation and a queasy sense of betrayal. 'He was a student, and a very able one too,' he said, recovering his courage.

The Political Organiser grabbed his arm and drew him closer. Misha tried not to recoil from the halo of stale sweat and ashtray breath. 'You show poor judgement, Citizen Petrov, and I understand your mother is an enemy of the people. But I am also concerned about your choice of subject matter for this class. *Richard II* could be considered counter-revolutionary, could it not? It was politically naive of you not to notice this.'

Misha's mind was racing. How did this man know about his mother? And it had never occurred to him that a play about the murder of a medieval English king might be counter-revolutionary. He felt an overwhelming urge to tell the Political Organiser that Shakespeare must have been able to see into the future, to write counter-revolutionary propaganda four hundred years ago, but he bit his tongue and waited to hear what this man would say next. Visions of smashed porcelain on his apartment floor and his terrified neighbour being dragged away from the *kommunalka* flooded into his head.

The grip on his arm loosened. 'You are young,' the Political Organiser said indulgently. '*Much Ado About Nothing* would be a better text to study. I saw it in the Realist Theatre a year or two ago. It was very funny.'

Misha breathed again and nodded his head rapidly. 'I am sorry for my political naivety, Comrade Organiser,' he said, trying to sound as calm and sincere as he could. The man smiled coldly and then left.

Misha hurried back to the metro and home. The mention of his mother had shaken him more than the warning about what he was teaching. If the Political Organiser knew, who else knew? He wanted to tell Valya about what had happened but he hadn't seen her all week. In fact, the last time he had seen her was the evening of the banquet. On an impulse, he dropped by the Golovkins' apartment at the Armoury and banged on the door. No one answered.

Maybe she was ill? He had been left to collect Galina Zhiglov on his own for several days and missed Valya's cheery ability to make conversation with the solemn little girl as he walked to her school.

He hadn't seen Valya around school either, so that night he asked his papa if he had seen Anatoly Golovkin at work.

'He's been away this week,' said his father.

'Is he all right?' asked Misha.

Yegor Petrov sounded increasingly impatient. 'It's nothing unusual. The *Vozhd* takes secretarial staff with him when he visits the republics. I expect Anatoly has gone too. I go sometimes, as you know. Why do you ask?'

Misha felt sheepish. 'I haven't seen Valya for several days. I wanted to know if she's all right.'

His father sighed. 'Valentina is a lovely girl. Of course she is. But you are like a little lamb trotting after its mother with that girl. You are too young for her. The sooner you realise that, the happier you will be.'

Misha blushed bright red. 'Papa!' he said indignantly. 'Valentina is just a good friend, but she likes me too. Can't you see that?'

Yegor's face hardened. 'Mikhail, you do not talk to me like that. Go to your room.'

Misha couldn't help himself. His anger boiled over. 'Maybe if you had cared as much for Mama, you would have done more to help her when she was arrested.'

His papa sprang to his feet and cuffed Misha hard on the side of his head, sending him stumbling backwards. 'Go to your room,' he said again, his cold, calm voice an eerie contrast to his violent action.

Half an hour later, as Misha was reading on his bed, still fighting back tears, there was a knock on his door. His father came in without waiting for a response. He was carrying a bowl of cold water and a small sponge, which he put on the bedside table. Then he sat down on the bed. Much to Misha's surprise he put an arm round him.

'I am sorry I hit you. This is not the way a respectable communist should behave.'

He felt the side of his son's head and wrung out the sponge. 'There is a little lump. Hold this here for a while. It will help. Do you want an aspirin?'

Misha shook his head. His anger was gone now and he just felt sad for them both. 'I'm sorry I made you angry,' he said.

'Never mind. It's forgotten.'

'I think of Mama often,' said Misha. 'Every time I open the front door I hope she'll be here.'

His papa hugged him tight. 'Mikhail, for both our sakes we should not speak of your mama.'

He got up to leave, then paused by the door. 'You should go to sleep now, Misha. I'm also sorry I hurt your feelings when I spoke about Valentina, but please think about what I said. She'll never be more than a big sister to you.'

Misha felt himself getting angry again and tried to hide it. He knew that if he tried to kiss her their friendship would end in an instant. But he wasn't going to talk to his papa about that. It was too embarrassing. He nodded and turned his gaze back to his book.

After reading a little longer, his eyes grew heavy and he switched off his reading light. As he drifted towards sleep, a sudden thought brought him rapidly awake. Had the NKVD come for Valya? She and he had often shared dangerous opinions. He dismissed the idea but it stayed there to nag at him. He would never betray her, but maybe there were others with whom she was just as indiscreet? And if they had arrested her, what would she say about him when she was interrogated?

He heard noises outside the door and his heart started to beat hard in his chest. *Don't be stupid, Misha,* he told himself. *That's just Papa.*

There was no sense in this at all. But then there was no sense in a lot of what the NKVD did.

He woke again in the early hours after a horrible dream. He was talking to Valya at the school gates and she was being pleasant but distant with him. Then, as she adjusted her hairband, he noticed all the nails were missing from her fingers. She carried on talking about an exam she was taking and he was desperate to ask her what had happened but the words would not come out. And when he looked at his own hands, the nails were missing from them too.

CHAPTER 7

Valya was not at school the following day either and no one he asked seemed to know what had happened to her. Again he knocked on her apartment door on the way home from school and again there was no answer. That evening he fretted alone with his thoughts and went to bed without seeing his papa.

Yegor Petrov came into the kitchen the next morning as Misha was preparing his breakfast. He looked exhausted.

Last night's meeting had ended at 2.30 in the morning, he told Misha. They had been caught up in an argument about German planes flying over Soviet territory. The subject seemed to bore the *Vozhd* but some comrades who were present seemed to think it was serious. Afterwards, Yegor was not asked to go on to Stalin's nearby *dacha* at Kuntsevo with the others. Stalin often asked his associates to go over there when the business of the day was completed. There was usually drinking and feasting and maybe a film, until at least four or five in the morning.

Yegor said he didn't mind being left out. 'I think Comrade Stalin could see how tired I was. You know, I felt sorry for the ones that were asked.' He told him the People's Commissar for Foreign Affairs, Vyacheslav Molotov, looked especially grey and fatigued, but no one in their right mind would refuse an invitation.

'He keeps such late hours at the *dacha*,' Yegor continued. 'Half the time it's just vodka drinking and farting contests. And he doesn't turn up at his desk at nine like the rest of us. We don't usually see him until the middle of the afternoon.'

Misha liked it when his papa told him these little secrets. He wondered if Yegor was making an effort to be nice to him after their argument a few days ago. He would try too.

'I shall fry you an egg,' said Misha and they sat and ate breakfast together.

As Misha drained his coffee cup, his papa asked if he would lend him a hand tidying the *Vozhd*'s office before he got on with his homework. Yegor had told him several times he would be able to get him a secretarial job at the Kremlin. Misha wasn't sure he'd like that. He admired his papa for doing the job he did but he didn't envy him.

He was always pleased, though, when his father asked him to help him with his work. There was something exciting about being in the great rooms where the Soviet leaders directed the lives of millions of Russia's citizens.

The office in the Little Corner was barely a couple of minutes away from their apartment. Yegor and Misha passed through the various layers of guards and office staff with little more than a nod.

They set about tidying the papers and filling the inkwells round the great baize-covered table in Stalin's office. Misha had helped his papa like this several times before but Yegor never left him alone with Stalin's papers. This time his father seemed distracted with tiredness. Misha couldn't quite believe it when his papa went into the room next door, leaving Misha on his own. He noticed a handwritten note with kisses by the signature in among the official government documents. For a fleeting moment he wondered if this was a note from a lover. The official story was that Stalin hadn't had a relationship since his wife had died ten years before. But there were rumours of a liaison with his maid at the Kuntsevo *dacha*. There were other rumours too, that his wife Nadya had not died of appendicitis, as reported, but had actually shot herself.

Making sure his papa was busy in the next room, he looked again more carefully:

Daddy,

I am pleased to tell you that your housekeeper was awarded top marks for her essay. I send a thousand kisses.
Housekeeper

The note could only have come from one person: Svetlana, Stalin's fifteen-year-old daughter.

There was a reply on it too, in Stalin's neat, instantly recognisable hand: *We send our congratulations to our housekeeper. Daddy, J. Stalin.*

Misha felt uncomfortable intruding in this intimacy. But he couldn't help feeling that the exchange seemed a bit childish too. Although Svetlana was well on the way to becoming a young woman, he'd noticed how Stalin still liked to pick her up and cuddle her and kiss her as if she were a young girl. It was one of the strangest things, seeing the all-powerful *Vozhd* cooing over his daughter. Maybe she sensed he still wanted her to be his little girl and played along with it. Misha had seen her flirting with Stalin's bodyguards when her father wasn't around. She could be disarmingly bold. Svetlana made Misha anxious. She walked the corridors of the Kremlin with the same assurance as Beria and even Stalin himself.

He continued to tidy the *Vozhd*'s large desk, thrilled at this peak into the inner workings of the great Soviet state.

He was guiltily glancing over a report on the increasing instances of German warplanes flying over Soviet territory when something else caught his eye. Among other papers casually scattered across the desk there was a sheet marked with the NKVD stamp and filled with spidery black scrawl. He could hear his father in an ante-room speaking on a telephone so he picked it up. A quick scan revealed it to be a confession. *Between 1938 and 1940 I colluded with the arch traitor Trotsky, and counter-revolutionary forces, deliberately sabotaging aircraft designs for our Yakovlev Yak-4 bombers . . .*

As his eye drifted over the document, Misha noticed a mark along the right-hand side of the sheet which he was sure was dried blood, and recoiled in revulsion. He heard his papa put down the phone so he hurriedly replaced the sheet where he had found it and tried to compose himself.

'You can go back to the apartment now, Misha,' he called. 'Get yourself ready for school.'

The afternoon passed in a blur. Misha felt too anxious to focus on his classes. The bloodstained confession kept intruding into his thoughts and he wondered if Valya had signed a similar one, full of traitorous things he had said to her over the last few weeks.

But when school finished at 8.00 that evening, she was

there at the school gates waiting. He ran up to her and took her hand. 'Valya! How are you?'

She looked pale and sullen. 'I've been ill, Misha,' she said. 'Will you walk home with me?'

'Of course,' he said, trying to contain his pleasure in seeing her.

There were several things he wanted to tell her about – like poor Vladlen at the automobile plant, and Svetlana's note to her papa – but not the confession. That was too dangerous.

Valya was so quiet he wondered if he'd done something to annoy her.

Eventually he told her about Svetlana and how she had got 'top marks' in her composition test. He thought that might catch her interest. 'I suppose she's spent her whole life being fawned over by people who want to get close to the *Vozhd*,' he whispered.

Valya nodded. 'I don't envy her future husband, whoever he might be,' she said in a monotone. 'Stalin will never forgive him for taking her away.'

'Yes,' Misha agreed. 'He wouldn't dare to step out of line with either of them.'

'Mind you, she likes you,' said Valya, cheering up for a moment. 'You've helped her out with homework a few times, haven't you?'

Misha blushed. It was true. She came to him when she had an assignment on Shakespeare to write. 'She's all right really. She just doesn't expect anyone to say no to her, and so far I haven't had to.'

Valya gave a hollow laugh. 'Play your cards right and she might be Mrs Petrov one of these days.'

Misha gave her a dig with his elbow. 'I'll start spreading rumours about you and Vasily Stalin, if you don't watch out! I know you've always had your eye on him!'

Valya shuddered and for a moment Misha thought he saw a tear brim in her eye. Stalin's youngest son, Vasily, was only a few years older than both of them but they had both heard awful stories about him propositioning girls on the secretarial staff.

She grew quiet again and their conversation ground to a halt. As they neared the Kremlin, she surprised him by hooking her arm around his, and they continued to walk the final kilometre home in silence.

She waited for Misha every day for the next week, although she did not call on him in the morning. She wasn't unfriendly but she was still subdued. And she did that thing again – hooking her arm around his when they reached the streets near to the Kremlin.

Misha knew she would be angry with him if he asked

her what was wrong. He was sure it hadn't just been an illness. He wondered if she'd fallen out with a boyfriend – someone she hadn't told him about. Or maybe there were arguments at home about her choice of university subject?

He tried a more oblique approach. 'How did you get on with that aeronautics exam? Have you had the results yet?'

She shrugged and smiled for the first time that week. 'Ninety-five per cent. Best in the class. Keep it up, they say, and I'll definitely get a place at the university.'

So it wasn't that.

Halfway up Ulitsa Serafimovicha she stiffened. 'Keep walking,' she muttered. 'Don't look round.' Misha could feel how tense she was but said nothing.

After a minute, she glanced over her shoulder and Misha could feel the tension drain from her body. He looked at her expectantly. She swallowed hard and nodded. 'Misha, let's go and sit in Bolotnaya Square. Somewhere away from people. I have to tell you something.'

So they did, and she sat right next to him and began to talk in a low voice.

'I was walking home the day after the banquet, one of the days when you were off teaching at the automobile plant, I think, and it was raining really heavily and I got soaked. Just as I got to Ulitsa Serafimovicha I noticed there was a big official car driving very slowly behind me. I ignored it but it stayed there matching my pace. Then it drew level and I could see a window opening. Someone said, "Get in the car," like it was an order. I turned to look and was all set to tell them to get lost when I saw it was Comrade Beria. I don't know if he'd realised it was me. Everything is a bit hazy when I think about it now. Maybe he thought I was just any young woman, but when he recognised me I think he decided he didn't care that I knew him. "Comrade Golovkin," he said. "It is a terrible afternoon, *devotchka*. May I offer you a ride back to the Kremlin?" Well, I was frightened of offending him, and I thought maybe he really did just want to give me a ride back, so I got in.

'I asked him how he knew my name and he told me he had seen me waitressing at the banquet. That made me feel uneasy and I could tell he'd been drinking. He offered me a cigarette and of course I told him I didn't smoke, then he grabbed my arm and tried to kiss me.'

Misha had seen this scene played out in films about life before the Revolution – most often with a beautiful peasant girl and a fat, lecherous landlord. The girl usually broke down in tears when she told the story to her brother or father, who would seek vengeance and end up being executed for defending her honour.

63

Valya continued her story in the same quiet monotone. 'His hands were all over me. It was vile so I just froze like an icicle. I didn't know what else to do. Maybe that made him think twice about what he was doing, or maybe it just put him off, and he stopped. We sat there in the traffic with the rain pounding on the roof. It was the longest five minutes of my life. Neither of us said anything. I could just hear him breathing. Long, angry breaths. Then shortly before the bridge he tapped the glass between the compartments and the car pulled into the side of the road. "You know what happens to anyone who tells state secrets, don't you?" he said. "Off with their heads, is what happens." Then he gave me the most horrible smile I've ever seen in my life and said, "Goodbye, Comrade Golovkin."'

'Oh, Valya,' said Misha. 'I'm so sorry . . .' He was lost for words.

'There's more,' she said. 'When I got out of the car, I caught a glimpse of Kapitan Zhiglov at the wheel. He was looking away – probably didn't want me to see him. But I was sure it was him. So that's what he does when he isn't beating up enemies of the people. I'll never be able to look him in the eye again.'

'We can tell him your routine has changed. I can collect Galina and then we can call round at yours on the way to school?'

She leaned forward and kissed him on the side of the head. 'Thank you, Misha. That would be very helpful. Now listen, you mustn't tell a soul what happened. "Off with their heads" – remember.'

'Have you seen Beria since?' asked Misha.

She nodded. 'I saw him in the corridor at the Armoury, later the same evening. He looked straight through me as if nothing had happened.'

Valya was shaking a little.

Misha took her hand. 'Valya, I wished I had never asked you to do that waitressing job . . .' he said.

'Misha, he's seen me around the Kremlin. He knows my father. He always gave me a creepy smile when he saw me. Honestly, it's not your fault.'

They walked home in silence, still arm in arm.

CHAPTER 8

Late May 1941

As the school year came to an end, Misha was pleased to see Valya looking more relaxed. Her exams were over and she was certain she had a place at Moscow University that autumn. Valya's dream of training to be a professional pilot, or even an aircraft designer, was becoming a distinct possibility. There had been no more trouble from Comrade Beria. She still wouldn't go with Misha to pick Galina up, but she had managed to greet Kapitan Zhiglov with a pleasant smile when they ran into him one day, although Misha did notice her hands trembling a little afterwards.

The sun was getting hotter by the day and they had the school holidays and the brief summer ahead of them. So for now they could look forward to a lazy few weeks and trips down to the Petrov's *dacha* at Meshkovo, to the south-west of the city. Maybe they'd even go swimming in the little lake there.

Misha and his papa had been getting along better too. In fact, Yegor Petrov had started telling Misha things he was sure should be confidential: odd things about the Germans, for example, and how the communiqués from the Nazi government were getting increasingly terse. Misha knew it must put them both at risk, but he supposed his papa told him because he did not have Mama around to talk to. He liked it though. It made him feel closer.

So now, as the spring turned to summer, he awaited his late-evening meals with Papa with a mixture of fascination and fear. What would he tell him next? In his heart he knew that Yegor Petrov was placing them both in danger by sharing these secrets with his son. Not that Papa wasn't careful. Every time they sat down to eat, Yegor would turn the radio up loud. Sometimes the upstairs neighbours would knock on the door and complain that it was disturbing their evening tranquillity.

Yegor told Misha he was taking precautions in case they were being bugged. Then he would change his mind and say, 'Why would they bother with a little minnow like me?' But Misha was glad of his caution. He had never heard of this 'being bugged' before. Being overheard – everyone in the Soviet Union knew about that. But 'being bugged' was something completely new. He hoped, as they sat side by side at the dining table, that their conversation was too quiet for any little microphones to pick up over the sound of the radio.

Misha had even started to look around the apartment. Every day now, since Papa first mentioned it, he checked when he came home from school. A vase of flowers, a bowl of fruit, the book that lay on the big bureau in the dining room – all of them were inspected. Misha was going to make sure that he and Papa did not go the same way as Mama.

That evening's meal brought further startling revelations. 'The *Vozhd* has lost his ability to tell right from wrong,' whispered Papa. 'We had some high officials from the air force in today complaining about the training aircraft they have to use. They crash far more frequently than should be expected. One of the air marshals lost his temper and said Stalin was making his pilots fly in coffins. There was a long silence and the *Vozhd* paced around the room. I knew there would be trouble because his eyes were darting around more than they usually do. Then he lit his pipe and said, "You shouldn't have said that." The poor man went white. I don't think we'll be seeing him again.

'Then after they left, the *Vozhd* started ranting about saboteurs deliberately damaging the planes, meddling with the engines. It was ridiculous. Everything is sabo-teurs, wreckers, foreign spies. And nobody, nobody dares to question anything. Nobody will ask, "Are the planes badly designed? Have we spent enough time test-ing them?"'

Misha wondered what on earth he should say. He remembered the bloodstained confession he had seen on the *Vozhd*'s desk but thought it wise not to mention it. When he looked up, he saw that his father's eyes were brimming with tears and he said, 'Sometimes, often, I wish we were back at the *kommunalka* and Mama and me were both still teachers. Misha, I had wanted you to join me working here – you're a bright boy after all – but I think you need to get as far away from here as possible. I don't know how it's going to end. I don't like to think about how it's going to end.'

On the final day of the school year, after they had had their reports and results, Misha and his friends arranged to meet in the Gorky Park of Culture and Rest at 8.00 that evening. There was an open-air dance on the side of the big lake there, in a fenced-off section, with a band and a bar. It was only four kopeks to get in, but Nikolay persuaded them to follow him round to the back of the enclosure, where there was a gap in the fence. 'We can all buy an extra bottle of beer if we get in for free,' he pointed out.

It was one of those soft early summer evenings, and Misha had the time of his life. At first he had been distracted because Valya had turned up with a young man from the flying club who he didn't know, and who she didn't introduce to anyone. In fact, she kept out of the way of them all that evening and spent her time with her date and his friends. But Yelena had danced with Misha all night. She knew all the latest Latin American steps, like the tango, that were popular in Moscow that summer. And she was good at the foxtrot too. It was all right to dance that now, although Misha remembered it had been banned as a bourgeois dance when he was younger. At the end, when the band played a slow waltz, Yelena had held him close, and they had even kissed, but then Nikolay and Sergey started to whistle and the moment passed.

They all walked home, their arms linked together, all of them declaring it had been a brilliant evening. Yelena smiled so sweetly when she said goodbye, and squeezed his hand.

Valya only spoke to Misha at the very end of the evening, after they had shed their other friends one by one on the walk back to the Kremlin. 'She's a nice girl, Yelena,' said Valya. 'Very pretty too. She's always liked you!'

Misha blushed. Valya sounded a bit tipsy.

'Who was the fellow who came with you?' he asked, trying to sound nonchalant.

'Oh, that's Vitaly. I know him from the flying club. I think he's quite good-looking, and he can be charming, but he's a bit too fond of talking about himself. He kept buying me drinks and I thought maybe he was trying to get me drunk. He offered to walk me home but by then I think I knew he wasn't really interested in me. I told him I had plenty of friends here to see me home. He seemed quite relieved.'

Misha wondered if she was disappointed or annoyed about it. Then she said. 'You know, for all this talk about women being the equal of men in our brave new Soviet world, I don't think many young men actually like women who are ambitious, or scientists, or pilots . . .'

She sounded quite crestfallen, which wasn't something he expected from Valya. But then she laughed and perked up. 'It would never have worked anyway. His name is Vitaly Ustyuzhanin. What a mouthful. I wouldn't want that name. And we'd be called Vitya and Valya – people would be forever mixing us up!'

CHAPTER 9

Early June 1941

Misha's evening mealtime conversations with his father grew more disturbing, so much so that he began to fret about Yegor's state of mind. He even put off asking him if he could have the keys to the *dacha* in Meshkovo to stay there a few nights with friends because he didn't want to leave his papa alone in the apartment. Sometimes he heard muffled shouting through the wall. It reminded him of when Mama and Papa used to argue and he quickly realised that Yegor was having nightmares and talking in his sleep.

One summer night, when Yegor had come home a whole two hours before sunset, he seemed particularly agitated. He could not sit down and paced around the room. As they ate, he fidgeted and could barely find the patience to chew his food. Eventually he turned on the radio and whispered, 'I have something so important to tell you. We must go outside and walk in the street as we talk.'

Misha nodded. It was a beautiful evening. Warm, slightly damp, the kind of twilight that made you wish you were at the *dacha* rather than on the stale streets of Moscow, breathing in the chemical smells from the factories and road repairs.

They walked out of the Borovitskaya Tower and on to the bridge across the Moskva. The rush hour was long over and there were only a few people crossing the bridge with them. Misha and his father stopped and rested on the stone balustrade and stared over the river at the Kremlin.

'Misha, what I tell you now you must never ever repeat . . .'

Misha's exasperation spilled out. 'Papa. I would *never* tell anyone what you tell me. I know that would be inviting my own execution, and yours.'

Yegor shushed him. Misha rarely spoke so brazenly to his father and he expected a clip around the ear at least. But this time Yegor looked at him with a mixture of tenderness and fear. 'Misha, my son, the Nazis are coming. I am sure of it. And if they come now, they'll be here before the winter.'

Misha gasped. 'Papa, that's treason. We have the greatest military forces in the world. How can this possibly happen? Haven't you seen that film *If War Should Come*? If

Hitler invaded, the working people of Germany would rise up and destroy him from within. It just won't happen.'

'You must know that's complete nonsense,' he said sadly.

Misha wasn't sure. He realised that he really wanted to believe it. He found it comforting. But really, deep inside, he knew it wasn't true. It was also the sort of thing Barikada would say and now he felt embarrassed. Yegor looked him in the eye. 'Viktor and Elena have gone to the western republics. We don't know what has happened to Mama. There is only you and me left. We have to know that we can talk to each other in confidence. You don't have to pretend with me. Even if they take me to one of Beria's torture chambers, I will never betray you.'

Misha let Yegor put his arm around him, like he used to when he was younger. He wanted to ask him about the envelope full of roubles, but he lost his nerve.

They carried on walking down to Ulitsa Serafimovicha, the route Misha always took on his way to school. Yegor said, 'Let's sit in Bolotnaya Square. There are seats by the fountain.'

Misha liked it there. Sometimes, when Valya was not with him, he would sit on his own and watch the fountain playing, watch the world go by.

Yegor looked sad. 'These people who pass us have no

idea what is coming. Every day we have reports coming in from spies in the Luftwaffe headquarters in Berlin, spies in the German Embassy in Japan, informers in the heart of the British government, and they all tell the same story. The Hitlerites are poised and ready to invade. Every night I think, *How can I tell Elena to get out of Odessa?* She's so close to the German border she'll be captured or killed in the first few days. How can I tell her, Misha, without the NKVD finding out and killing me? And Viktor in Kiev. He'll be in danger soon enough.'

Misha didn't know what to make of it all. 'But if you are so certain,' he said, 'and all the others who come with these reports, why is Comrade Stalin doing nothing about it?'

'Who can see into the head of the *Vozhd*? I can guess at one of twenty things he might be thinking. Maybe he thinks just the one thing. Maybe he thinks all twenty. My guess is that he thinks there are wreckers and saboteurs, trying to get the Soviet Union to declare war on Germany so the Nazis will have to fight. That's plainly ridiculous. But I think Comrade Stalin believes Hitler is a sensible man. He thinks he must realise the Soviet Union is too big, too powerful, to conquer as easily as all those little countries in Europe. Hitler gobbled them up in days – well, a few weeks for the bigger ones like France – but he must know the Soviet Union is different.

'But there is one thing that really worries me, Misha. You know how we attacked the Finns soon after the war began in Europe? What they never told the people was that the campaign was a catastrophe. We won a small victory in the end – some territory around Lake Ladoga – but we could not conquer that little country despite our overwhelming size. There have been so many generals taken away, never to be seen again. The army is like a headless behemoth. We have a few good generals left, but not enough. Most of them are too frightened of the *Vozhd* to do anything other than obey every instruction meekly, even if it's completely crazy. You can't run an army like that. You need leadership. You need initiative. And if our army defends our country as ineptly as they attacked the Finns, then the Germans will be in Moscow in a matter of weeks. They might even be here before the first frosts.'

Misha couldn't believe his ears. His lazy summer was evaporating before his eyes. 'Papa, what makes you so sure? About the invasion, I mean.'

'There's just too much intelligence to ignore. Reconnaissance flights into our airspace. Troops massing on the borders – especially dense around the River Bug. "Training exercises," says Stalin. "They're ready to invade," I want to scream. There's only one general who will speak openly with him about this – that bastard

Zhukov. He's a brute, but you have to admire his courage. Just today he was telling the *Vozhd* he was convinced the Hitlerites were coming, and Stalin said, "You want a war, don't you, Comrade General? You want a war so you can be promoted to even higher rank, and strut around with even more medals on your chest." Well, Zhukov was flabbergasted. I think we all were. How can you reply to that? It's a level of debate you'd hear in a school playground.'

As his father became more frustrated, Misha could only listen, occasionally looking round to see if anyone was close enough to eavesdrop.

'And the worst of it is he seems to be permanently drunk these days. When I give him his papers when he gets to the office around four in the afternoon, he just stinks of alcohol. It's on his breath, coming out in his sweat. He must know something is up, but he can't admit it to himself. And what really breaks my heart is, I look around at these people in our beautiful city, and I think of all the sacrifices we've made to build our Soviet state, and it's all going to be for nothing, because our great leader will not take a blind bit of notice of what all his comrades are telling him.'

The next morning was Rest Day and Misha was looking forward to a leisurely breakfast with his father. But although it was a brilliant summer morning, and the sun was streaming into the apartment, he still felt anxious about their conversation the previous night.

There was an impatient knocking at the door. Yegor shrugged. It couldn't be work. The telephone usually summoned him to emergency meetings.

Misha went to open the door. It was his mother's younger sister, Aunt Mila. She had been a regular visitor before Anna Petrov had disappeared. Anna and her younger sister would huddle together and talk quietly to each other in rapid sentences. Mila was always rather cold to Yegor, but that changed once Anna disappeared. Even now, nearly a year later, she still came to visit, walking an hour from the Sparrow Hills, refusing to use the metro. The Kremlin guards usually recognised her and waved her through.

Misha liked his aunt and never minded his visits to the Sparrow Hills to help her with her little garden. He'd seen her several times walking the streets of Moscow talking to herself, though, and today she seemed more pale and confused than usual.

'Mila, what has happened?' said Yegor. 'You look terrible.'

She sat down, uninvited, at the dining table and waved her hand. 'Misha, make me some coffee, my dear,' she said. 'I need something to keep me awake. I barely slept last night.'

Yegor took her hand. 'So what can we do for you, Lyudmila?'

'Yegor, you know I dream a great deal, and in my dreams only the dead come to visit me . . .'

'You have told us this,' said Yegor. Misha could tell his father was trying to be kind, but he still picked up the impatience in his voice.

'Last night I dreamed of Anna . . .'

Misha's ears pricked up.

'. . . We were sitting in a concert hall. She was waiting for her piano recital to begin, dressed in a cream gown. She had been practising all month and she was very nervous. But no one was there. It was just the two of us. She was on the brink of tears. "I thought Mama would come," she said . . .'

Mila choked her words and Misha felt strangely upset with this overheard conversation. What on earth was Aunt Mila talking about? His mother played the piano, that was true. But only in a rudimentary way – enough to bash out a Pioneer marching song or 'The Internationale' in a school assembly. He hurried with the coffee and returned to the dining room.

'Lyudmila, why trouble us with such a story?' said

Yegor. Misha could see that he was very angry – perhaps more angry than the story warranted. 'Why bring poor Anna to mind? You know how sad it makes us to think about her.'

Aunt Mila gripped his arm. 'Yegor, you know when I dream it is only the dead who come to visit me. I know without a doubt that Anna is dead.'

'Lyudmila, you are trying my patience,' said Yegor, his voice rising in anger. 'I have my single Rest Day from work and I want to enjoy my relaxation and let my thoughts drift to pleasant things.'

Misha tried to calm things down. 'Auntie, it's only a dream. Dreams don't mean anything.'

Aunt Mila sat tight-lipped. She had gone whiter than ever.

'I don't believe you are right, Lyudmila,' said Yegor firmly. 'We were told plainly by the NKVD that she had been placed in custody with no right of correspondence for ten years. I am sure she will be back here one day.'

Misha's aunt gasped in horror. 'Are you sure those were the words?' she said. 'You have never told me this.'

'Mila, you know we have to be careful,' Yegor said gently. 'We all have to be careful.'

'Yegor, I will be indiscreet with you, as you have been with me. I have a neighbour. She had a boyfriend who worked for the NKVD. He got drunk sometimes – no, a lot. You could hear him, shambling about upstairs, sometimes roaring with laughter, sometimes shouting. I don't think I ever saw him sober. But she told me he'd said "no right of correspondence" means they have shot their prisoner. It's a little joke they have. Like saying a prisoner is "going to a wedding". They say that when they're taking them out of Moscow to execute them.'

Misha reeled with horror and the blood drained from his face. He collapsed into a dining chair.

Yegor shouted then. 'Lyudmila, don't upset the boy, and don't talk nonsense. How can you talk such nonsense?'

Lyudmila's eyes darted around the room, as though she were looking to escape. 'I trust you are right,' she said starchily and sipped her coffee, wincing a little. Misha hoped she would get up to go. But she didn't. Instead she bowed her head and smiled. 'I am sorry. I know I have tried your patience. So tell me, Misha, how are you faring at school? I hear you are quite a scholar. Your mama was a clever girl too . . .'

Yegor answered for him. 'Misha is helping the workers at the Stalin Automobile Plant with their reading.'

'We're reading Shakespeare, actually, Papa. I talk to the ones who can read already,' said Misha.

His papa shrugged it off. 'He takes after his mother, you can see.'

Mila seemed more relaxed now. She sipped her coffee, peered out of the window and said, 'I must go before it rains.'

When she had gone, Yegor blew a long stream of air through his lips. 'Misha, we both know Lyudmila is rather detached from the world. I wouldn't take anything she says seriously. Not least what she said about Mama being shot.

'And that piano nonsense,' he continued, before Misha could ask him any more about it. 'You know Mama only played a little. We had the chance to have a baby grand piano – do you remember, when we first moved here? They asked, as there was one available, and Anna turned them down.'

Misha remembered all too well. He had wanted to learn to play himself and had felt angry with his mother for several weeks afterwards for depriving him of the opportunity. But he was puzzled why his father felt the need to remind him. And he was irked at his refusal to talk about Aunt Mila's fear that his mother was dead. He didn't seem particularly concerned about any of this. In fact, this whole conversation didn't really make sense.

CHAPTER 10

21st June 1941

Bright sunlight burst through the narrow gaps in Misha's curtains and as he woke he was pleased he did not have to go to school that day. He was glad to be at home most of the time, not least because he continued to worry about his papa. Yegor seemed to be in frequent pain and told his son he thought he might have a stomach ulcer. Misha urged him to see a doctor but he wouldn't hear of it.

'Plain food is what I need,' he said. So they ate scrambled eggs and tinned tomatoes and cucumber salads. Misha developed a craving for steak, which he would occasionally satisfy with a lunchtime fry-up.

He was relieved that his papa had not told him anything more about the Germans since that night at the start of June. Nothing had happened since. It must just have been a rumour which got out of hand in the Kremlin. The other day he had read an article in *Izvestia* denouncing rumours of war as 'totally without founda-tion' and 'lies and provocations'. Misha was beginning to think he'd get his lazy summer after all.

Today he thought he would ask his papa for the keys to the *dacha* in Meshkovo and see if Nikolay, Valya, and anyone else they could round up, wanted to catch a train out there and spend the day in the forest. If they left at eleven, they could arrive with a picnic lunch. It would be good to make the most of the warm weather. They would get home at dusk carrying bags bursting with summer fruits from the garden of the *dacha*.

He had heard his papa get up earlier and guessed he had been at his desk in the Little Corner since 9.00 a.m. When Misha headed over to talk to him, he found Yegor Petrov looking pale. Misha worried that his stomach condition might be worse. Instead, Yegor whispered, 'There are all sorts of bizarre things happening this morn-ing. German cargo ships are setting sail from our ports – even ones that have not yet loaded the goods they came to collect. And we've had reports from the fire brigade that at the German Embassy they are burning all their documents. We've been trying to contact the *dacha* at Kuntsevo but Comrade Stalin has given strict instruc-tions that he's not to be disturbed.'

'What do you think is going on?' Misha whispered

back. He couldn't believe his papa was discussing this with him in the office. He had a horrible sinking feeling in his stomach.

'I think the Hitlerites are about to attack us,' said Yegor wearily. 'I don't want you to go to Meshkovo. Once the attack starts, they will send aircraft to bomb the cities. I don't know what the range of their aircraft is. Maybe we are too far away – but why risk it?'

Misha realised now that the terrible rumours about Germany were actually true.

'You know, during the war against the Whites I was fighting down in Tsaritsyn and we were caught on a troop train,' said Yegor. 'Two fighter planes attacked us, and we were trapped in a wagon. When you're fighting out in the open, you can always hide or throw yourself to the ground. On that train we were rats in a trap. There was a hailstorm of bullets and splinters and shards of glass. I was lucky; I escaped with a few cuts, but men right next to me were killed.'

His papa had rarely talked about the Civil War before and had brushed off Misha's questions when he'd plucked up the courage to ask. Now, for the first time, he began to understand why.

'What shall we do?' Misha asked. His mouth had gone dry. He was desperate for a drink of water.

'Wait. I can suggest nothing else.'

So Misha went back to the apartment and read Chekhov's *Three Sisters*. That was playing in Moscow at the moment and he had wanted to see it later in the week. As the morning wore on, he went round to the Golovkins to ask Valya if she wanted to have a picnic with him in Gorky Park. She was pleased to see him and eager to get out of the Kremlin. She asked him to wait while she changed into a floral cotton dress.

'Dmitriy might be there. I don't want him to see me looking dreary!'

Misha sighed to himself. She had told him about Dmitriy – a boy she knew from the *Komsomol*. She'd taken quite a shine to him and kept hoping he'd ask her out. She came out of her room wearing a red ribbon around her thick curly hair and Misha thought she had never looked more beautiful.

They walked along the broad avenue on the southern side of the Kremlin down to the Borovitskaya Tower. They noticed an unusual amount of activity for a lunchtime on Day Six. Officials were hurrying to and fro between the office buildings, clutching box files and sheaves of documents. Every one of them looked harassed or anxious.

A cool breeze blew off the Moskva as they walked

over the great bridge and Misha felt hungry. They bought black bread, salami and apples from a little grocery store on Bolshaya Yakimanka and reached the Park in a little over twenty-five minutes. There was an empty bench overlooking the Moskva Embankment so they sat there in the sunshine.

Misha was bursting to tell her what Papa had said but knew he couldn't. He could think of nothing else to say. It was Valya who broke the silence between them. 'I know you're dying to tell me something, Misha, so I will spare you the torment. I know what's about to happen.'

She waited for a young woman with a pram and two tiny children to walk past.

'Papa says the whole Kremlin knows the Nazis are about to invade. Only Comrade Stalin denies it. But he knows something is wrong too.' She paused. 'I wonder how long it will be before they get here.'

Misha felt slightly disappointed. He thought he'd known something Valya didn't.

'You sound so certain that the Nazis will be successful,' said Misha. 'Papa told me Comrade Stalin says the Germans won't attack because they know it will end in failure. He says that anyone with a rational mind will see this. And although the *Vozhd* hates the fascists as much as any good communist, he thinks the Nazi leader is a shrewd character. He has made some clever moves in Europe.

'He has a magnificent army,' Valya said.

'Yes, but Napoleon had the best army in Europe too,' said Misha, 'and that ended in catastrophe when he invaded Russia. We've all seen the pictures of *der Führer* at Napoleon's tomb when he went to inspect Paris last year. Hitler admires the little Emperor as much as any warlord. He'll know what happened to Napoleon's army, and if he forgets, I'm sure his generals won't tire of reminding him.'

Valya let out a long sigh. 'Or maybe they're as frightened of him as our generals are of the *Vozhd*?' She hooked her arm around his. 'I'll tell you a secret. Don't ask how I know.'

It was obvious how she knew. Anatoly Golovkin must have told her. Just as his papa did with him.

'That campaign in Finland, after we reclaimed our territory in Poland. It was a disaster. Russian corpses were piled up like pyramids, frozen in the snow. The Finns beat us! A little country hardly anyone has heard of.'

'But we won, didn't we?' said Misha.

'Barely. D'you know what Papa told me? Oops, I've told you where I heard it now . . . He said the Finns used to attack when the Soviet troops were having their afternoon rest. Completely inflexible. And our soldiers were starving half the time because supplies didn't get delivered. If the Finns can do that to the Soviet army, then we don't stand a chance against soldiers who conquered Europe in just a few weeks.'

'So much for our treaty with Germany!' said Misha. 'I was there at the banquet to celebrate it. It was only two years ago. I can't believe they're going back on that after such a short time. And even if they were stupid enough to attack, we're much bigger than the other countries. We're huge. We have far more soldiers and far more tanks and aircraft. There are twenty thousand aircraft in the Soviet air fleet.' Misha was trying to convince himself. He finished with a flourish. 'And we're Russians!'

'Misha, Papa says Comrade Stalin has had most of the top army men liquidated. Tukhachevsky, Yakir, Primakov . . . All those heroes of the Soviet Union we used to hear about and see on the podium in the Red Square parades, we don't see them any more. They're gone. Almost certainly dead.'

'Rokossovsky came back,' Misha said.

'They must have decided he was more useful to them alive. But most of the generals and divisional commanders now are new men. They're terrified of doing the wrong thing and they'll be hopeless against experienced Nazi commanders.'

A cool breeze blew off the river and she shivered in her thin cotton dress and pulled him a little closer. Her body was touching his, from shoulder to feet. He felt her warmth and a hopeless longing but glancing at her face he saw she was staring forlornly out to the far embankment.

'What can we do?' was all Misha could think to say.

'I'm going to join the partisans,' Valya said firmly. 'They'll be asking for volunteers to fight behind the German lines.'

'Then I will too,' said Misha rashly.

She hit him briskly on the arm.

'You, Mikhail Petrov, are not old enough. But you could join the air defence section of your *Komsomol* detachment. I dare say they'll put you in charge of a Pioneer brigade.'

'Look at this city,' she continued. 'All the effort, all the work we put into building it up since the Revolution. All these factories, all these new hospitals, apartment blocks, they're all in danger. You know what the Nazi bombers have been doing to London.'

'Papa says the bombers could be here tomorrow,' Misha said.

'No. They'll need to set up airbases nearer to us.' She paused again and looked him straight in the eye. 'But they'll be here soon enough.'

CHAPTER 11

Midnight, 21st June 1941
Polish–Soviet Border

Augustus Grasse breathed in the damp summer air that drifted across the River Bug. Grasse shivered a little and lit another cigarette, carefully hiding the light in the slit trench he had dug that evening.

'Hey, me too, *Dummkopf*,' said Steiner, holding out an unlit cigarette of his own. Both of them were soldiers in Generalfeldmarschall Fedor von Bock's Army Group Centre, Fourth Army, 197th Infantry Division.

They were both from Berlin but Grasse didn't really like Steiner. He was always banging on about the Jews, how they had started the war and how they would soon be getting what they deserved. Grasse wanted to tell him he sounded like a parakeet, parroting that poisonous Dr Goebbels. But he bit his lip. Grasse, the boy whose father was a communist, a traitor to the Reich. He just had to put a foot wrong and the Gestapo would be bringing him in for interrogation.

On the far bank of the River Bug were the Russians. At least he assumed they were there. His division had been perched in their start position for several hours now and they had not heard a whisper from the other side. The Germans had even brought up their tanks – there was no hiding the thunderous rumble the Mark IV Panzers made – and the smell of exhaust still hung in the night air like some monstrous creature panting and sweating after a night's marauding.

The simple truth was, Grasse wanted the communists to win. As an eleven-year-old he had joined his father fighting the Nazis in the street battles in Berlin, before Hitler wangled his way into power. When the Nazis got in, his father was one of the first to be sent to Dachau. He came out five years later. Augustus didn't recognise him – he was skin and bone, and bald. That fine head of black hair had disappeared, and his bushy eyebrows had gone white.

'Get out, son. Go to Russia, or France,' his father had said, shortly before he died of tuberculosis. 'The devil has come to Earth.'

But Augustus didn't go. He didn't know the right people to bribe for a visa, and he knew instinctively that he had to keep his head down, otherwise they'd come for him too. So he went along with all the military training at school. Some of it he even enjoyed. No one could throw a grenade quite like him. He had a silver cup on the mantelpiece to prove it.

Augustus never forgot his father's politics. It made perfect sense. Power to the people. From each according to his ability – to each according to his needs. There was almost a religious logic to it. Didn't Christ want to help the poor and oppressed to make a better life for themselves? He looked at his watch. They were four hours away from H-hour. *Barbarossa*. The greatest invasion in history. That's what the Division Colonel had told them earlier that evening. Why couldn't they have posted him to Norway or the Afrika Korps?

Steiner finished his cigarette, coughed, spat noisily, and said, 'I need a crap.' He hauled himself out of the trench and disappeared into the bushes behind them. 'Don't step on a mine,' whispered Grasse, half wishing he would.

In an instant a mad idea gripped him. *Let them know.* Let them know the Wehrmacht was coming. Let them know millions of soldiers and thousands of tanks and aircraft were about to pour into the Soviet Union and destroy their army. Grasse weighed up his chances. It was entirely possible he would die in the morning attack. And he didn't like to think what the odds were of him still being alive when they reached Moscow. If he went

94

over, the Russians would treat him like a hero, and he'd get out of this whole mess. Once he told them he was a communist too, or at least his father was, then they'd sort him out a cushy job, surely?

The worst that could happen was that he'd spend the war in a prisoner of war camp. He fumbled in his pocket for his hip flask and took a long drag of schnapps. Then he hurriedly removed his combat jacket and webbing. He took one last look around to see if Steiner was coming back, then gingerly made his way to the water's edge. Slipping silently into the cool water he began to swim towards the other side.

Grasse emerged on the eastern bank of the River Bug dripping wet and shivering uncontrollably. The water had been colder than he had expected, and even as he swam he had begun to regret his decision to desert to the Soviet side.

He was sure the noise he made as he clambered up the bank, trousers swishing against his legs, water dripping from his shirt, must have drifted back across the river, but no one on the German start line seemed to have heard. His companion, Private Steiner, had noted Grasse's absence but hadn't yet realised that he had gone for good.

Grasse stumbled on into the darkness, expecting to meet Soviet troops at any moment. But there was nobody about. He carried on hurrying east, desperate to make contact with the Russian soldiers before the invasion began and he was overtaken by his own side. He hadn't thought that through. He'd be shot for desertion, without a doubt. Maybe he'd be the first German soldier to be executed in this campaign. That would be something that would have made his father proud.

He heard a town clock chime 1 a.m. and headed towards the sound. Within half an hour he had reached a small village where he heard Russian voices. In the moonlight he could see horses and a few motor vehicles and realised this must be a detachment of Soviet soldiers. There was a small group of them clustered around a field kitchen, and he called out as he approached, 'Comrades! Don't shoot.'

A moment later he found himself staring down the muzzles of several rifles. Instinctively raising his hands above his head he spoke slowly, in German. 'Comrades, I must talk to your officer. Very urgent.'

The soldiers muttered rapidly to each other. Clearly no one here spoke German. Grasse noticed with alarm that one of the men was fixing a bayonet to his rifle. The soldier advanced towards him but beckoned Grasse to crouch on the ground.

He muttered a single word to him, like a man talking to a dog, and another one of the soldiers ran off into the darkness.

Within ten minutes the man returned with an officer. He had a smarter uniform and looked more intelligent than these peasant soldiers.

'Who are you?' said the man in poor but comprehensible German.

Grasse snapped to attention.

'Augustus Grasse of Generalfeldmarschall Fedor von Bock's Army Group Centre, Fourth Army, 197th Infantry Division. I have urgent news. My division, indeed the whole German army, is about to invade your country. Please be prepared.'

Grasse didn't expect what happened next. The officer hit him so hard it knocked him over. 'You are lying.'

'No, no, comrade,' shouted Grasse. 'Please, you must believe me. My division will cross the Bug at four this morning.'

Kicks rained down on him, on his back, in his groin, in his stomach. One of them connected with his head and he could feel blood in his mouth. He thought a tooth had come loose.

'Please, comrade,' he spat out. 'I am a communist. My family has suffered enough already under Hitler. I am here to help you.'

The beating stopped. Through the pain and bewilderment, he heard voices shouting at each other in Russian. Then the officer spoke to him again. 'I will contact my senior commander. If you are lying, I will kill you myself.'

Augustus was taken to a cellar room and locked in. Then the lights went out. He crawled his way to the door and politely called for a drink. He flinched when the locks from the door opened and blinding light spilled in. Three Soviet soldiers beat him some more. When they left, he noticed through the shaft of light under the door that there was a tin mug on the floor with water in it.

Alone in the dark he listened for the quarter-hourly chimes of the town clock, and sank into despair as each chimed off the time to the invasion. Shortly after 3.00 a.m. the door opened and light flooded into the cellar again. Two Soviet soldiers called him up the stairs. When he reached the top, one of them grabbed his hand and twisted it behind his back. The other then bound both his hands together with a piece of rough rope. Grasse was surprised when a blindfold was hurriedly tied around his eyes. These Soviets were keen to keep things secret, he thought. He was swiftly ushered outside; he could tell by the drop in temperature and the warmish night breeze that blew over him. Night air, it was so delicious. He prodded his loose tooth with his tongue. It had stopped bleeding. Maybe he wasn't going to lose it after all.

Then he heard someone shouting – a barrage of what he guessed were orders. He imagined they were going to take him to talk to a senior officer, maybe even a general. He listened out for the sound of a car engine, but the last thing he ever heard was the crack of six rifles in a firing squad.

CHAPTER 12

Misha lay awake for much of the early hours staring at the ceiling. He hoped desperately that his father and Valya were wrong about the Germans, but in his heart he was sure they were right. Eventually he drifted off but woke to the sound of a ringing telephone. He dimly remembered hearing his father come home sometime in the middle of the night, and had assumed Stalin had had one of his usual late-night meetings. But this telephone call was definitely unusual. The dim light filtering through the drawn curtains told him it was barely dawn.

He got up to see his father looking exhausted in his dressing gown. 'Papa, are you all right?' he asked.

Yegor nodded. 'I have to go. Something has happened. Comrade Stalin is meeting the Politburo in half an hour.'

'Do you think the Germans have invaded?'

Yegor beckoned Misha to come into his arms. He

hugged him tight. 'We have to be brave, Mikhail. This will be our greatest ordeal.'

Misha made his papa a coffee as he dressed, then sat with him as he ate a hurried breakfast. He left the apartment at five thirty and told Misha he would probably have to cook his own supper. He would try to let him know when he would be back but, whatever happened, Misha was not to come to the office and disturb him.

As soon as Yegor left the apartment, Misha turned on the radio. He could get nothing from the Soviet stations, so he turned the dial to see what else was being broadcast. Amid the foreign babble he heard city names close to the German border, like Minsk and Odessa, and wondered at once if they had been bombed. Elena, his sister, lived in Odessa. On one radio station he recognised the language as German and the announcer seemed unnaturally strident and excited as military brass-band music played in the background. This time he heard 'Kiev', where Viktor lived, and realised that if all three of these big regional cities had been targeted this must be a massive attack.

Misha felt sick with worry. It was still only six o'clock, so he went back to bed and drifted into an uneasy sleep. Outside he could hear the rumble of cars and lorries. There was a lot of coming and going inside the Kremlin walls. He dreamed of Valya marching off to war dressed as a commune worker and carrying a Simonov rifle. As her squad passed by in a big Red Square parade, she saw him in the crowd. She turned and shouted something he couldn't hear.

He woke again around eight and this time it was fully light. The sky was overcast and appropriately glum. Misha wondered if it was too early to go over to see the Golovkins. There was a knock at the door and he knew at once it was Valya. She was wearing the same cotton dress she had worn the day before, with a blue cardigan.

'I have some pastries,' she announced, marched boldly in, and threw the bag down on the table.

'Papa was summoned at five o'clock,' she said.

'My papa too,' said Misha.

'I'm going to volunteer immediately. Will you come with me?'

'They won't have me, Valya. I'm too young.'

'I don't mean for you to sign up, Misha. I don't want you to go to the front. It's going to be very dangerous, and yes, you are too young. Most of us who go will probably not come back, but I can't sit here and wait for the Hitlerites to arrive. I have to do something.'

'What does your papa say?'

'I'm not going to tell him.'

'Valentina, if I go down there with you and he finds out, he'll be furious with me.'

'Misha, I'm going anyway. Come if you like. Don't come if you don't like.'

They ate their pastries in silence. 'All right, I'll keep you company,' said Misha, 'but let's just see what's going on on the radio.'

This time the Soviet stations were broadcasting. One of the announcers told everyone to be prepared for a very important broadcast at midday.

'Let's go out into the street,' said Valya. 'We know what it'll be about. But this is history. This is something we'll remember for the rest of our lives – whatever's left of them!'

'You're brave,' said Misha – half in mockery and half in admiration.

'Actually, Misha, I'm terrified.' She laughed nervously. 'Make yourself look presentable. We might be in one of the newsreels, looking stoic and heroic. I'll meet you back here at half past eleven.'

Valya turned up in her red dress this time, with the matching red ribbon in her hair. Misha wore his best tweed jacket. She took his arm. They walked out of the Kremlin at Trinity Tower and up Gorky Street, which was packed with grim, anxious people, many huddled together in small groups of friends or family, their arms linked together. Strident brass-band music was playing through the street tannoys, not unlike the music Misha had heard in the Nazi broadcast, but this was entirely unusual for a Sunday morning. Eventually the music stopped and the crowd's dull murmur turned to a frightened silence.

Misha expected to hear Stalin, so he was surprised when a hesitant Molotov started to speak.

'Citizens and citizenesses of the Soviet Union. Today at four o'clock in the morning, without a declaration of war, German forces fell on our country . . . an act of treachery unprecedented in the history of civilised nations . . . The Red Army and the whole nation will wage a victorious Patriotic War for our beloved country, for honour, for liberty . . . Our cause is just. The enemy will be beaten. Victory will be ours.'

Misha and Valya stood close to each other and seemed to be the only ones there who weren't surprised. People seemed shocked and upset, and some had tears streaming down their faces.

When the announcement ended, Misha and Valya walked up Gorky Street to the Military Recruitment Office to find there was already a vast queue.

'I'll come back tomorrow,' Valya decided instantly.

Instead they wandered on through the streets.

'Valya, I think you are wrong about the Germans getting here in a few weeks. Did you see the people? They looked anxious, of course – who wouldn't? – but they looked like they were going to fight with everything they've got. They looked like they were willing to fight to the death. If I was a German in Moscow, one of the diplomats, there must be some of them left, I'd be terrified. I'd be thinking, "What have we stirred up?"'

Valya looked unconvinced. 'Maybe, Misha, maybe. But you can't stop a tank with stubborn courage. You need something more than that.'

They listened to the conversations in the street but most people seemed to know very little – 'Our army will destroy them. The war will be over in a month.' Or, 'I have heard our soldiers have already seized Warsaw!' So far they had heard nothing bad about the government – you wouldn't expect that in a crowded street. When they rounded the corner of Tverskoy Boulevard and Ulitsa Gertsena, they saw a crowd gathering by the tobacconist's. An old lady, dressed in a shabby coat and wearing a woollen headscarf despite the warm weather, was haranguing a group of passers-by.

'This is God's punishment on us all,' she shouted. 'Famine, forced labour, mass murder. God has turned his back on us. And so has Comrade Stalin. Why did he not give the speech? Why did he not speak to his people?'

One man was clenching his fists and looked white with anger. 'How dare you talk like this when our Revolution is so threatened?'

Other people in the crowd were jostling her. 'Get stuffed, you mad old cow,' said one.

But worse was coming. Two Militia men were shoving through the far side of the crowd. Much to Misha's surprise Valya immediately stepped forward and grabbed the old lady by the arm. 'Come on, *Babushka*, you cannot say things like this to people. Let me take you home.'

The woman looked startled, then angry, but just at that moment she too saw the Militia men and flinched. Valya turned to face them and addressed the whole crowd. 'Comrades, this misguided old lady is my grandmother. I have come out to look for her and take her home. Please ignore her ramblings. She has not been herself since her husband died.'

The mood of the crowd changed. 'Keep her locked in, the mad old bat,' said one young man. But he sounded indulgent rather than angry.

'Come on, *Babushka*,' said Valya, and tugged on her arm. The woman shrank, her anger gone, and she began to walk down Ulitsa Gertsena. Misha could barely stand to watch. The Militia men looked undecided. Was this mad old lady worth their time and trouble? They walked towards them and Misha's heart sank. He wondered whether to intervene but knew this could easily make things worse.

Instead he tagged behind. One of the Militia men grabbed the woman roughly by the arm. 'You, you old sow, what have you been saying?'

Valya turned and looked him straight in the eye. 'Comrade, my grandmother is unwell. She has these episodes. I am taking her home.'

The other Militia man was right behind. Misha recognised him. He was one of the two who had spoken to them back in the spring when they had stopped to help the boy who been run over.

He spoke to the other man and then turned to Valya. 'Very well, young lady, you may take her home. But keep a close eye on her. We will have to take her away if this happens again.'

When he was sure the Militia were out of sight, Misha caught up with them. 'Valya, what on earth are you doing?'

The old lady turned on him at once. 'Aren't you a gallant young man?' she snapped. 'Fortunately you have a very brave girlfriend.'

'No, *Babushka*,' said Valya. 'He was right to stay out of this.' She was looking flustered and her hand trembled a little. 'Do you remember the tall one, Misha? He stopped us when we helped that boy.'

She turned to the old lady. 'Where do you live?' she asked.

The woman looked fearful. 'Are you NKVD?' she asked.

'*Babushka*, do we look like NKVD?' said Valya.

The old woman shook her head.

'It's not this way,' she said. 'Strastnoy Boulevard.'

'*Babushka*, forgive me, but you should keep your opinions to yourself,' said Valya. 'Especially at a time like this.'

The old lady looked dejected. 'I feel so angry, and sometimes I just snap and it pours out. I know it's stupid but I can't help it.'

They walked on in silence, and when they reached Strastnoy Boulevard she said, 'Come up to my apartment. I want to thank you.'

CHAPTER 13

Misha and Valya let their curiosity get the better of them. The old lady led them to a grand building overlooking a tree-lined square and they walked up a linoleum staircase to a small apartment facing out on to a dark courtyard. The old lady bustled around her kitchen, talking as she fetched cakes from a tin and prepared a pot of coffee.

'My name is Antonina Ovechkin. You may call me Baba Nina.'

Misha didn't quite know what to make of this. He called his own grandmother *Baba* – Nana – but it seemed a bit overfamiliar for someone they didn't know.

Valya seemed comfortable with it. 'Baba Nina, you put yourself in terrible danger there.'

'Yes, but it's over now. So don't fuss about it,' she said sharply. Then she softened. 'I do have a terrible temper, I know. But I get so impatient with people. They just swallow everything they hear. They're like sheep.'

Valya didn't want to have a conversation like this with someone she barely knew so she changed the subject. 'Do you live alone here?'

'My husband was a colonel in the Red Army,' she replied. 'He gave his whole life to the Revolution. And now he's disappeared. He was on Tukhachevsky's staff. They all vanished. You saved me, just then. If they'd arrested me, they would have checked my file and that would have been it. If they didn't kill me, they would have sent me to the camps and that would have done for me, just as surely.'

Baba Nina talked for an age about her grandson Tomil, who she saw only once a month because her son was so busy, and how good he was at walking, and how he had started to say his first few words.

But she asked them about themselves too, and what they were doing with their lives. When Valya told her she wanted to be a pilot, Nina said, 'A fine ambition for a Soviet girl. But I wish they would make our planes safer to fly. D'you know half our pilots are killed in training?'

Valya was unperturbed. 'I know how to fly already, Baba Nina. I learned with the Pioneers and the *Komsomol*.'

As they were leaving, she grabbed Valya's arm and said, 'I might be old and a bit cranky, but I still have friends. You are one of my friends now.'

110

By the time they walked out into the street, it was mid-afternoon and the overcast sky had cleared a little. It was trying to be a pleasant summer day. 'Old people like to talk, don't they?' said Valya. 'I imagine she spends a lot of time on her own. You can tell she used to be important though, don't you think? She has something about her.'

As they walked back to the Kremlin, they passed long queues outside every shop that sold food.

After a while, Misha said, 'That was a brave thing you did, Valya. You could have been arrested.'

'I wasn't going to let those Militia men beat up an old lady in front of my eyes. Of course she was stupid to talk like that in front of everyone, but could you have walked away while those thugs laid into her?'

Misha didn't like to admit it, but he could have done, quite easily. He didn't say anything.

Valya leaned closer. 'And I thought she made at least one good point. Why was Molotov making that speech? Comrade Stalin should have had the courage to speak to his people.'

Valya went to volunteer for partisan work the next day. Misha asked her to reconsider – she must know she would be murdered by the Nazis if she was caught. They took her name and details and told her to return home to await further orders.

Misha volunteered for air-raid duties and was given training in aircraft recognition. The German bombers looked far more sophisticated than anything the Soviets had.

Valya had been right about the bombers and Yegor Petrov had been wrong. There were air-raid drills in that first week but no bombers appeared in the sky over Moscow. The Nazis were still out of range. But Misha had an awful sinking feeling he would be seeing those angular, sinister-looking planes from the training manuals all too soon.

Misha barely saw his father in those first few days of war. Yegor Petrov came back in the middle of the night, and when he rose, usually around eight in the morning, he hurried immediately to his office in the Senate block without having breakfast.

It was almost a week after the invasion when Misha finally sat down with his papa to eat together. He looked haggard and Misha was pleased to be able to cook him a meal. 'I cannot tell you how terrible these last few days have been. The *Vozhd* has been shouting and bullying everyone. Even that tough old bastard Zhukov burst into tears. The Hitlerites are five hundred kilometres into our territory – in less than a week. Minsk has gone, and Vilnius . . . Odessa is threatened. They expect Smolensk to fall within a week. And the worst of it is, he won't let the soldiers retreat. We've lost *half a million men* in a week! And our so-called great air force . . . a *thousand* planes destroyed on the first day! On the first day . . .'

His voice petered out, lost in despair. Then he spoke again.

'What will happen to Elena? If only I could have warned her.'

'She might have got out, Papa. Maybe she's on a train heading to Moscow with Andrey.'

'Mikhail, I tell you now, I never liked that husband of hers. I sometimes wondered if he had anything to do with your mama's disappearance.'

Misha felt queasy. He would never be able to look Andrey in the eye again.

Yegor waved his hand dismissively. 'I don't know. It's just a feeling. A whisper to the NKVD about something she'd said, that was all it took a couple of years ago. I think Andrey would betray his own mother if he thought it would advance his career.

'So I don't really care what happens to him. But I am desperate to hear about Elena. Especially as I don't think the lives of civilians are a concern to the *Vozhd*. All our efforts are concentrated on our military resistance.'

Life went on almost as normal for the first few days of the war. Misha met up with Nikolay, Yelena and other friends from school, often in Gorky Park or for strolls along the embankment next to the River Moskva. When the weather was good, they would go to the chess corner in the park and while away the afternoon playing on the chess sets that were set out there. They talked of friends and relations who had marched off to the distant front line and their hopes for a speedy victory. So far none of them had heard of anyone being killed. The papers gave no hint of the casualties in the areas where fighting was reported. There were air-raid drills almost daily in Moscow, but no bombers arrived.

Yelena had smiled a little bashfully when she saw him again. Misha felt guilty about not calling on her in the weeks since the dance, but his heart wasn't in it and he didn't want her to get the wrong idea.

Apart from the air-raid drills and training in the air defence squad there was not a great deal for Misha to do. They did manage a day trip to the Petrov *dacha* at the end of the first week of July, but even Nikolay failed to cheer them up when he revealed a bottle of vodka in his knapsack on the train down to Meshkovo. It seemed wrong to be enjoying themselves with such an impending catastrophe looming on the horizon.

They arrived just after midday and Misha gathered twigs to get a fire started in the kitchen stove, so they could boil water for coffee. Nikolay had not been before and he shamelessly nosed around the place. 'Treasonous . . . formalistic . . . petit-bourgeois . . .' he called out with mock disdain when he saw the Petrov children's paintings and drawings on the living-room wall. 'Unquestionably the work of wreckers and saboteurs.'

'Leave him alone!' laughed Yelena. 'They are all exemplary displays of proletarian culture.'

Misha smiled to himself. She was joking too, he was sure.

Valya laid out a picnic of tomatoes, pickled cucumber, ham and black bread on a tablecloth on the patch of grass in front of the *dacha*.

Nikolay looked at the spread before them with barely concealed admiration. 'What a wonderful feast!' he said. 'I haven't seen ham in the shops for months.'

'Papa rescued it from the office,' Valya said with a wink. 'It was going to be thrown away. And when she was alive Mama made enough pickled cucumber to last until the twenty-first century.'

As they sat in the dappled light of the forest, enjoying the warm summer afternoon, Misha sipped slowly at the shot of vodka Nikolay had poured for him. He resisted the urge to down it in one when Yelena called for a toast, 'To our certain victory.'

He had to be especially careful not to let slip to his friends how much he knew, and he noticed how reticent Valya was too. It wasn't that he didn't trust them, but who could guarantee that one of them wouldn't blurt out, 'Misha told me . . . and his father works in the Kremlin'? That would get back to the NKVD, he was sure. Then there would be a hammering on the door in the middle of the night. Both he and Papa would be taken away.

But listening to them talk as they ate he could tell his schoolmates had already mastered the art of decoding the news from Soviet State Radio. They had realised how rapidly the Nazis were advancing towards Moscow as the names of the cities where 'Red Army soldiers heroically repulsed the invaders' grew nearer.

A little over a week after the invasion, the great Belarus city of Minsk had fallen. Dvinsk and Riga had also been taken. There was fighting in or close to Kiev and Smolensk.

'Just looking at the map you could tell they'd come

three hundred kilometres in the first few days,' said Nikolay.

Valya said, 'If they keep going at that rate, they will be here within a month.' Then she remembered. 'Misha, isn't your sister Elena living in Odessa?'

Misha nodded. 'And Viktor is in Kiev. He must be in great danger too. We have heard nothing from either of them.'

Valya shivered, despite the warm summer sunshine. 'It's like one of those horror films from America, like *Frankenstein* or *Dracula*, where the villagers are waiting. Waiting for the monster to arrive and destroy them.'

'I fear for you too, Valya, going off to join the partisans,' said Nikolay.

'I'm not sure I could volunteer for something like that,' said Yelena.

The others all muttered their agreement.

Valya put her arm around Yelena and gave her a brief hug. 'I'm still waiting for instructions. The sooner I go, the better. I need to do something to keep me busy.' She laughed. 'Better than just sitting around waiting for the worst!'

Misha could understand that. 'I never thought I'd miss school,' he said, 'or think the holidays went on too long.

All my workers' classes have been cancelled too now we're at war.'

Valya turned serious. 'That's why I want to join the partisans. I think if you go and do some training, then join a fighting unit, you can at least feel like you are making a difference.'

They left the *dacha* in the late afternoon and returned to Moscow. After they had said goodbye to the others at Bryansk Station, Misha and Valya walked back to the Kremlin in silence. When Misha got to his apartment, the door was unlocked, which meant Papa must be home. Something must have happened.

He was in the kitchen, pouring a glass of vodka. He turned and beamed, and sank his drink in a single gulp. 'Misha! Great news! Elena has escaped from Odessa. I don't know what has happened to Andrey, but she is heading east by train. There was a postcard waiting when I got back from work.'

'Where is she going, Papa?' asked Misha.

'I don't know. At least she is out of immediate danger for now.'

'I wonder what will happen to Viktor?' asked Misha.

'I think Viktor will join the partisans. He used to tell me he thought the treaty with the Nazis would never

118

last, and said that's what he would do. I hope he gets away before the Nazis arrive. I have read reports saying they have been shooting Party members on sight. Right there on the roadside if they find them carrying their Party cards.'

Then he looked his son straight in the eye. 'Misha, if the war continues like this, they'll be here before the end of the summer.'

After that, Yegor disappeared for another week. Misha did not see a sign of him, not even around the Kremlin grounds, and after a few days he began to worry about what had happened. He went to the Golovkins' apartment and asked Valya if she'd seen much of her father.

'He's been at work every day, sometimes only home for a few hours. I will ask him about your father,' she said.

She came round a couple of hours later. 'Misha, your papa is all right, I think. My papa says he is with Comrade Stalin in the *dacha* at Kuntsevo. The Kremlin staff haven't been able to speak to the *Vozhd* for several days. He isn't taking calls and your papa is the one who has to tell everyone this.'

She stayed for a coffee.

'Have you heard more about your enlistment?' asked Misha.

Valya looked irritated and Misha wondered if he should not have asked.

'They won't have me. I got a letter this morning. I am to join the military air force and train to be a pilot.'

'Why are you so glum, Valya? You love flying.'

'I want to do something now, Misha. This waiting around while the Nazis are destroying our country . . . I can't bear it. I'll have to wait a few months before they decide on a posting, then there'll be further training, then who knows? I'll probably have to fly the mail around in Omsk or Novosibirsk. Or deliver fighters or bombers to the pilots who are actually going to fly them against the Hitlerites.'

'You must be patient,' said Misha.

She got up and cuffed him around the ear. 'If that's the best you can do, I'm going.'

'Valya, I'm glad you're not going to fight with the partisans. I don't think I'd ever see you again if you did that.'

She looked at him.

'Little Misha. There are a lot of people neither of us is going to see again by the time this is over.'

Misha spent his evenings at his air-raid post on top of the Hotel Metropole. He was on a rota with other Young Pioneers and *Komsomol* recruits and sometimes he worked all night. When this happened, he was grateful there was no school; he would sleep until two or three in the afternoon. Then one day, just after an evening duty, he heard the door. Papa had come home.

Yegor looked grey with exhaustion but he managed a smile. 'Come and sit with me. I will tell you good news.'

Misha eagerly sat down at the dining table. 'The *Vozhd* is back,' said Yegor. 'I have been with him for a week at Kuntsevo. He seemed to be in a stupor. I was told to tell everyone who rang that he was unavailable. No phone calls, no visitors. I've had half the Politburo screaming at me. And half the Red Army generals. I was in despair. This is no way to run a country at war. Yesterday Mikoyan, Beria, Molotov, they all came down. I could tell Comrade Stalin thought they were going to have him arrested, but they begged him to come back. I was there, standing in the corner, wishing I was invisible. But he's back now. Things are going to change. I think everything is going to be all right.'

CHAPTER 14

Late July 1941

Posters of a severe young woman in a red headscarf, index finger to her stern, tight lips, had appeared all over Moscow. *Don't chatter*, it said in large angry letters, and *Be alert. In days like these, the walls have ears. It's a small step from gossip to treason.*

Misha squirmed whenever he saw that poster. He and Valya gossiped all the time, and his papa often told him things he knew he shouldn't be hearing. But how else were you supposed to find out what was really going on?

It seemed strange carrying on with normal life when terrible things were happening. Misha kept thinking of those thousands of planes, destroyed on the runways before they'd even taken to the sky. Like squashed flies on a windscreen. How could their forces have been so unprepared? How could they possibly drive away the Hitlerites when so much had already been destroyed? Papa had said little about the course of the war recently, and had swiftly scolded Misha when he'd asked. Perhaps Yegor felt he had said too much all ready? So Misha just did what everyone else did – listened to the radio to hear where the Red Army was fighting its latest 'heroic defensive actions'.

There was always school work to be done, even in the holidays, and Misha was determined to carry on with it. The German bombers had come a month after the war began, and air-raid sirens went off almost every night now, any time from dusk to dawn. It made everyone exhausted and bad-tempered from lack of sleep. It was even difficult to sleep during the day as the Kremlin grounds were full of carpenters putting up fake wooden buildings to try to disguise this most desirable of targets. When Misha wasn't on duty with the air-defence cadres, he would see how much work he could get done before the sirens went and they had to hurry to the air-raid shelter.

As he tried to settle to his homework one evening, Misha heard a determined knock at the door. He thought it might be Valya but when he swung back the heavy wooden door the *Vozhd*'s daughter Svetlana was standing there. He had not seen her since the very first days of the war, and he had heard she had been sent away from Moscow, to protect her from the danger of bombing. Misha had met Svetlana several times before and had always been very wary of her. He'd heard the children of other Kremlin families whispering that she was a spoiled, capricious child.

'You're back,' he blurted out. She looked different. A bit more grown-up now, more of a young woman. It was barely a couple of months since he had noticed her 'housekeeper' message to Stalin. He couldn't imagine her writing like that any more. She looked distracted too. The usual glint of mischief had vanished from her eyes.

'Comrade Petrov,' she said in a quiet voice, 'I have come to ask for your help.'

Misha was astonished. She had never addressed him in this way before. Or with such respect. 'Call me Misha,' he said. 'Everyone else does. How can I help you?'

She lowered her head. 'Please may I come in?' she asked. This was unprecedented. When she had seen him before, she had burst in through the door demanding his assistance.

'Of course, come and sit at the table. Shall I make you a cup of tea?'

She sat down and placed her heavy bag on the table. Misha called out to his father. 'Svetlana is here to pay us a visit.'

Yegor came in and immediately began to make a fuss of her. She explained that she had returned from Sochi, on the Black Sea, to spend a few days in Moscow before they decided where to send her next. 'I want to be here with Papa, and to share the danger,' she said. Misha felt a sudden flash of admiration for her, something he had never felt before.

'And what can we do for you?' said Yegor, who had taken over the preparation of the tea.

'It's Mikhail I've come to see,' she said. 'Misha's fame as a Shakespearian tutor continues to grow. I have an essay to write for my literature teacher. He wants to know what I think about *Antony and Cleopatra*. I have to explain the meaning of a speech.'

'I shall leave you two to get on then,' said Yegor, as he poured three cups of strong brown tea. He brought two cups over, then disappeared back to his study.

Svetlana smiled and fished a book out of her bag. 'It's the speech about the evening, the night sky. I've got to explain it in ordinary terms.'

Misha loved that speech. He wished he could read it in English but he barely spoke a word – just a couple of phrases: 'How are you?' and 'Thank you'.

'Aren't you learning English?' he asked Svetlana. She nodded but seemed distracted. 'If I help you, will you do me a favour too? If you can find the English edition, will you read it out to me, so I can hear how he meant it to sound?'

Misha could tell by the way her eyes darted around that she was taken aback by this request. Clearly Svetlana was not used to trading favours. But she managed a smile. They talked about the piece, how a 'promontory' was a mass of higher land or land jutting out into the sea, and how 'black vesper's pageants' meant the beautiful sights and sounds of evening. Misha thought, as he explained, how well his own teacher had taught him. But he also noticed how little attention Svetlana seemed to be paying to what he said. She was there but her mind was somewhere else.

'You look worried,' he said carefully. 'I hope everything is all right.'

She looked around, wanting to make sure she was alone in the room. 'Comrade Mikhail,' she whispered. 'We have known each other for some years. Our papas are old friends. I must talk with someone I can trust. Can I trust you?'

Misha nodded and wondered what on earth was coming next.

She fished around in her leather satchel, and pulled out a magazine. Misha had never seen it before and the typeface was completely indecipherable to him. He recognised the squiggles – they were the Western-style alphabet – 'Roman' it was called – but he understood it about as much as he understood Egyptian hieroglyphics.

'Are you allowed such things?' he blurted out. Misha knew anything at all from the West was regarded with deep suspicion by the Soviet government.

'Of course I am,' she said indignantly, barely keeping her temper. 'I am studying English. Papa asks me to talk to visitors from England when they come here. But look at this I read today.' She turned to a page where Nadya Stalin, holding Svetlana as a toddler, peered out at the reader from a black-and-white photograph. Misha could see a likeness with her mother, especially now Svetlana was growing older. Svetlana looked very cross in that photograph, although Misha thought it best not to mention this.

'Look at this,' she said quietly, reading out the caption and translating as she went. '*Stalin's wife Nadezhda Alliluyeva, pictured here with their daughter Svetlana. Nadezhda, known as "Nadya", is thought to have shot herself in 1932.*'

'But she died of appendicitis,' said Misha. 'Everyone knows that.'

Svetlana did not return his gaze. She stared hard at the photograph. Misha noticed for the first time her clear pale skin and light red hair. She was turning into a beautiful woman.

'She never liked me much, you know. Look how uncomfortable I look in that photograph. But I think she had a difficult life. I think she probably did shoot herself. Papa never speaks of her. I've learned not to mention her.'

'This is capitalist propaganda, made to make your papa look bad,' Misha said. 'You should ignore it.'

'No, I don't think so,' she said carefully. 'This is the *Illustrated London News*. It's a reasonable magazine. I've read it a lot and they seem to tell the truth in their reports. And the British are our allies. They have other articles here about how bravely our soldiers are resisting the Nazis, and how determined Papa is to lead his country to victory. Why would they put something like this in? Just out of spite? No, I think it's true. I think Papa drove her to it. I think she was so cold with me because she was so unhappy with him.'

Misha daren't voice an opinion, even if he had one, which he didn't.

Svetlana picked up on his discomfort. She placed a hand on his arm. 'I'm sorry to weigh you down with my own troubles,' she said. 'I ask you to tell no one of what I have said.'

'I promise you as a good communist never to repeat what you have said,' Misha hurriedly replied. There was an awkward silence. Then he said, 'Shall we get back to Antony's speech?'

She shook her head. 'No. You have told me enough,' and began to gather her books and notes.

'Here, come and walk with me to the embankment,' she said. 'It's a lovely evening.'

It was an odd request but Misha didn't mind. Maybe she felt she didn't want to part company from him quite yet, after confiding in him.

So they walked over to the grand avenue overlooking the Moskva River and stared into the opalescent dusk. The air was thick with the last of the hot summer day and swallows circled high above them. 'It's beautiful out here,' said Misha, looking down at the river and the handful of pedestrians that hurried along Kremlyovskaya. In the misty gloom you could barely see the buildings along Sofiyskaya on the opposite bank of the Moscow River.

For a moment or two they stood side by side, almost touching. Misha thought of Valya's teasing and hoped Svetlana didn't take a fancy to him. He was beginning to like her but having her as a girlfriend would be like going out with a scorpion. He reassured himself that he was too much of a lightweight for the daughter of the *Vozhd*.

The undulating mechanical wail of the air-raid siren cut through the dusk. 'They're early tonight,' she said calmly.

Misha and Svetlana watched a crowd of officials and secretaries heading for the newly built shelters in the squares and gardens of the Kremlin. They all walked at a steady pace to their allotted shelters, no one looked too concerned. After all, sometimes the sirens went off and nothing happened. He wondered whether he ought to escort Svetlana to her own shelter or wait for her to dismiss him.

But then they heard the faint buzz of aeroplane engines, swiftly blotted out by the steady thud of anti-aircraft guns. The Germans were here already.

'They've sneaked through in the fog,' said Misha, trying to keep the fear from his voice. The shelter the Petrovs had been allocated was close to the north wall. The first bombs were beginning to fall – a regular *crump crump* CRUMP – as the planes discharged their loads in rapidly approaching detonations. Sometimes there was just that single chain of explosions. Often the sound of crumbling masonry followed on.

The last explosion was close enough for them all to see the flash, and from the corner of his eye Misha saw black fragments hurling through the air. Svetlana grabbed him by the arm. 'Come to my shelter,' she said. 'It's nearer.'

All at once they were running, like everyone around them. Stalin and his cohorts had their own place of safety, newly dug just outside the Little Corner, close to the *Vozhd*'s own apartment and office. The two soldiers guarding the stairway entrance let Svetlana and her guest past without a word.

Misha noticed immediately that this was a different class of shelter. There was a crowd of excited, anxious people, but there were nowhere near as many as packed into the other Kremlin shelters. In place of the usual whitewashed concrete walls, and the faint smell of damp earth and human waste, there was a polished woody smell from dark panels and varnished parquet flooring. Immediately to the right of a large steel door he could see an operations room, just like the one in the Little Corner which he had helped Papa clear up after meetings, with the same map on the wall, and portraits of Lenin and Stalin.

The steel door clanged shut, and Misha wondered about the two guards, there on the other side. A loud explosion broke overhead and the lights momentarily flickered. People held their breath and Misha could see the tension on their faces. He felt perfectly safe – far safer than usual. He was sure Stalin's own shelter was deeper and altogether better than everyone else's.

Close to the operations room was a dining room with a long table set with a lace cloth and crystal glasses. There were other rooms too, either side of the long corridor, with closed doors. Misha and Svetlana hurried down to the large room at the end of the shelter. The room filled up rapidly and Misha looked around, recognising many of the Soviet leaders. Molotov was there, and Rokoss-ovsky and Beria. Then all at once, he saw Stalin staring straight at him. The eyes bored into him, holding his gaze, even as the *Vozhd* drew on a cigarette, his face unsmiling. Misha wondered if this was what a mouse felt like just before it was swallowed by a snake. He seemed to be saying, 'What are *you* doing here?'

Stalin broke off his staring and leaned towards a large burly man and whispered in his ear.

'Svetlana, do you think we should tell your papa that you asked me to come down here with you?'

'Don't be silly, Comrade Mikhail,' she hissed. 'Why should I bother Papa with insignificant tattle like that?'

The assistant was walking towards Misha with a purposeful, frankly hostile look on his face.

There was a deep and ominous rumble. The ground shook. Everyone stopped talking. Then the lights went and everything was pitch black. 'Comrades, please stand where you are and stay silent. The lights will return in a moment,' said a commanding voice Misha didn't recognise.

In the dark Misha felt a hand clutch his. He was sure it was Svetlana.

More explosions followed, including one close enough to dislodge earth and plaster and cause a few people to start coughing. Misha felt horribly vulnerable there in the dark and squeezed the hand that held his.

After an eternity, the lights flickered back on and people began to move out into the corridor. As Misha's eyes adjusted to the brightness, he realised Svetlana was no longer by his side. The sirens began to wail again – the steady all-clear signal this time.

He was anxious to leave, before the angry-looking man found him, and he shuffled out with the others streaming to the staircase exit, careful to keep his eyes to the floor. Outside, the first thing Misha noticed was the smell of burning, then that gas and sewage smell that always accompanied an air raid. Over by the north side of the Kremlin he could see flames rising above the rooftops, and the taste of water vapour from firemen's hoses mingled with the Moscow summer evening. Misha ran towards the fire.

'Go back,' said a guard as he neared the flames. 'One of the shelters has had a direct hit.' He was relieved to see it wasn't the one Valya and his papa used.

Misha dodged an ambulance as it swerved up the

central square and walked in a daze to the great road in front of the cathedrals to look south over Moscow. Although there was a total blackout in force, the city was peppered with fires. He thought about what Valya had said about who would still be alive when the war was over and a cold shiver passed through him. Sirens and alarm bells from ambulances and fire engines brought him back to the present and Misha remembered immediately that he should go off to his own *Komsomol* air-raid detachment to see what he could do to help.

CHAPTER 15

Early September 1941

August passed in a haze of air-raid sirens, Nazi bombs falling on the city and a procession of further dreadful news from the front. Now, whenever his friends met, he would hear of casualties. Nikolay had lost a cousin. Yelena had an uncle who had been killed near Orsha. He and Papa waited for news from Viktor and Elena, but there was only an ominous silence.

When Misha crossed the great bridge, he noticed work had started again on the Great Palace of the Soviets on the embankment. They had been building it for years on and off, and he had heard rumours that the foundations were not strong enough to support its huge size. But now it was going down rather than up. You could hear them on the site around the clock. The papers reported the steel girders used to build it were being turned into tank traps.

By the time Misha returned to school in early September, the German army seemed unstoppable. In the far north, the great city of Leningrad was surrounded. Down in the south, they had reached the Black Sea and it could only be a matter of days before the Crimea was occupied. Krasnograd and Novgorod had fallen. A mere two hundred kilometres lay between the Nazis and Moscow. As Nikolay had pointed out, rather alarmingly, it was a distance a fast car could cover in a couple of hours. Misha had realised how dangerous the situation was when he'd heard Kapitan Zhiglov had sent his daughter Galina to Kuybyshev, far off to the east. Lydia the maid had gone too. There was some natural justice in that. She had to put up with a difficult child, but at least she would be safe too.

Misha had also heard an extraordinary rumour about Stalin's eldest son, Yakov. He had been captured in the fighting around Smolensk and the *Vozhd* had had his wife and children arrested. Misha's mama had been friends with Yakov's wife, Yulia, and he remembered her a little. When he mentioned it to his papa, Yegor Petrov looked merely uneasy, rather than shocked. 'It's a standard procedure when a soldier surrenders. The *Vozhd* has to be seen to be fair.'

Misha shook his head in disbelief.

On the first day back in school, Misha's year were all assembled for a special extraordinary meeting. Misha sat with Nikolay and Sergey and was pleased when Yelena chose a seat as far away from him as possible on the other side of the hall. As he looked around, he noticed how many of his fellow pupils were looking unwell. Even twelve weeks into the war many had clothes that were starting to look too big for their bodies and the wan, malnourished look of street beggars. Clearly, rations for the general population were not as generous as they were in the Kremlin. He wondered if anyone would notice he wasn't looking any thinner.

'What's this meeting about, d'you think?' asked Nikolay.

'Probably some information on air-raid drills and other wartime procedures,' said Misha. He was starting to feel restless when Leonid Gribkov walked in and called the hall to order.

'Why's the Komsorg doing this and not Barikada?' whispered Nikolay. Barikada usually led the school meetings and they had both seen him in class, but he had seemed unusually quiet. 'I thought he'd be loving this,' said Nikolay. 'His chance to shine.'

Gribkov did indeed go through the air-raid precautions, and who was to muster where in the event of an attack. A series of names were read out, including Misha's, who was to act as air-raid warden and who was to take a register after an attack. He also reminded them all that the war office was still recruiting volunteers to defend

Moscow and to go into the occupied areas as partisans. It was not compulsory to do so, unless you were eighteen years old, but his clear inference was that younger volunteers would not be turned away.

Then he called for volunteers among the older students to replace teachers who had gone to fight. Misha caught Yelena's eye when Gribkov asked for a show of hands, and she had raised hers too. She smiled and gave him a thumbs-up.

Then Gribkov turned more serious than usual. He began to talk in the kind of political clichés that made most of the students gaze into thin air, about the pre-Revolutionary bourgeoisie – the factory owners and the landowners – and how they had tried to 'throttle the Revolution with the bony hand of hunger' and how even after their final defeat they had carried on sabotaging Soviet industry. He announced it was time once again to 'tear off the mask of the enemies of the people'. Misha wondered where on earth this was going and worried that he was about to be denounced. But then Gribkov turned and pointed directly at Yelena, and called her 'a wolf in sheep's clothing'.

Misha remembered what Valya had said about not being able to walk by when someone needed help. Amid the catcalls and boos directed at her he stood up and cried out,

'Yelena Rozhkov is an exemplary communist and works directly for the good of all Moscow people. I have known her for many years and have heard her speak nothing but good of Comrade Stalin and the Soviet Union.'

The room fell silent. Gribkov scoffed. 'Comrade Petrov, we know you and Rozhkov have an intimate relationship, and you are acting out of kindness. You do not know the facts I now have before me and you would be well advised to remain silent.' He was on a roll now, scenting blood, and he twisted the knife further. 'Your attitude is incorrect, especially for a member of the *Komsomol*. You should not be showing pity to the daughter of enemies of the people.'

Gribkov boldly announced that Yelena's parents had been factory owners in Kharkov before the Revolution and were exploiters of the toiling classes. It had also been discovered that three of her cousins, who had fled after the Revolution, now lived in Berlin and, it was assumed, were directly assisting the Hitlerites in their war of subjugation.

'Yelena Rozhkov, you are a non-person,' he announced. 'You are denied further education. Never return to this school.'

Yelena ran from the hall in tears, dodging the fists of some of the bolder students and Misha and Nikolay deliberately stood in the way of some who were rushing over with cruel animal glee to land a blow on her. Then they tried to find her but she had fled.

Misha had barely given a moment's thought to non-people before his mama had been arrested, and he was ashamed now that he had felt no more than a momentary flicker of pity. His earlier school days had been full of occasions where a girl or a boy was made to stand in front of the whole school and have their Pioneer scarf snatched away from them because they had been unmasked as the offspring of a 'non-toiling element'. Then the child, often bewildered and sobbing in shame, would be expelled from the school.

He'd sometimes see them later, hollow-eyed and begging in the street, the son or daughter of a former priest or noble or factory owner. He'd see a parent he recognised from the school gates cleaning a public lavatory, with that same haunted look. None of his schoolmates ever stopped to talk to these non-people, even if they'd been friends with them in the past. He and his comrades at school had all agreed that these factory owners had done the same thing to the ordinary workers before the Revolution. The rich and powerful had treated the people with scorn, and now they were only receiving natural justice for centuries of repression.

He burned with shame to think how easily he had

accepted these unmaskings. Especially now that he was keenly aware that only his father's position in the Kremlin had stopped the same thing happening to him. When Mama went, her arrest had been kept quiet. Misha had told his schoolmates his mother had fallen ill and had been taken to a sanatorium on the banks of the Caspian Sea.

The next Rest Day, Misha went to Yelena's home. Nikolay and Valya had wanted to come with him but he had persuaded them to let him go alone. It made no sense to put all their futures at risk.

The Rozhkovs lived in a small apartment near his Grandma Olya. Her parents were quite elderly and worked at the office of the People's Commissariat of Heavy Industry. They were 'prominent people', although Misha was sure they would now both have lost their jobs. He knocked on the door and was half surprised to hear movement behind it. A frightened voice called out, 'Who is it?'

Yelena's mother pulled back the door a crack. She looked as though she had been crying. 'You are lucky to find us, Mikhail,' she said, opening the door to let him in. 'We have to move out in two days, to a *kommunalka* in the Sokolnichesky district.'

'I'm sorry,' said Misha. 'Can I help you with your packing?'

141

'Anton, he wants to help with our packing,' she cried out to her husband, suppressing a hysterical laugh. 'Mikhail, we can only bring one suitcase each.'

Misha looked around the apartment aghast. It was comfortably furnished and full of books and ornaments and paintings. They would have to leave behind almost everything they owned.

'I just wanted to tell Yelena how sorry I am that this has happened and that I wanted her to keep in touch,' Misha said.

Yelena's father had come to join them. 'She always had a soft spot for you, Mikhail, and that is a very touching gesture. I wish you could tell her that. I wish I could too . . .' He clenched his jaw as he fought back his emotions. 'She has gone to fight with the partisans. She told us if she did that, then nobody would be able to accuse her of being an enemy of the people.'

Misha felt as if he had been kicked in the stomach. He told the Rozhkovs how sorry he was that this had happened to them, then he left. He managed to walk two streets before he had to sit down in a doorway and fight back his tears.

After the terrible first day, it was a relief to be back at school. The routine kept Misha occupied. He was pleased to discover that Valya would also be coming into school a couple of times a week to teach physics to the younger classes while she awaited her call-up to the air force.

Misha had also volunteered to teach literature to the younger ones, but he found that far more difficult than his classes with the factory workers. The children were too restless and could not understand why they should take an interest in Chekhov and the comings and goings of nineteenth-century aristocrats and merchants.

'Forget the Chekhov,' Sergey told him. 'You should try Tolstoy. *War and Peace* – Napoleon's invasion and what happened to his army. That'll make them sit up and take notice.'

In the next lesson Misha read them an extract depicting Napoleon's disastrous retreat through the Russian winter.

'And that is how we shall defeat the Hitlerites!' Misha announced triumphantly. The class cheered. This was what they wanted to hear and from then on he had their full attention.

After class, he hurried to the school canteen, keen to share his success with his friends, although his heart sank a little at the thought of what there would be to eat. Having spent the summer enjoying the usual provisions of the Kremlin elite, Misha had been particularly shocked by the sudden decline in quality of the school meals. They had always been bland but but now they were almost inedible. On his first day back there was a thin gruel for lunch that was barely more than hot water with potato peelings in it, and a few other unidentifiable vegetables. He thought longingly of the beautiful chicken soup his mother used to cook, with its tender meat, and sliced carrots, always cut on the horizontal – 'They look nicer that way,' she used to say, – and a good sprinkling of dill in the delicious salty broth.

Today's lunch was probably the vilest thing Misha had eaten that year. The meat was almost entirely gristle.

What's this?' said Nikolay. 'Lizards' gizzards?'

They all laughed quietly at that. The potatoes were full of black spots and the cabbage was stone cold. Worst of all was the gravy – a lukewarm glutinous paste which had traces of skin on top that reminded Misha of flaking brown paint on a damp wall.

'Is this the sort of thing you get to eat in the Kremlin?' said Barikada coldly. They were never going to be friends but Barikada had been especially distant with him from the first day back at school.

Misha thought about taunting him, telling him about the roast goose they had eaten yesterday, left over from a Kremlin banquet for visiting diplomats from the British

Embassy. But he understood why Barikada was angry, and he didn't want to make his friends feel bad either.

'The Soviet leaders share the people's hardships,' he said, and felt like a creep.

Barikada gave him a look of burning hatred. Misha averted his gaze. He wanted to tell him to be careful. But it would sound as though he were threatening to denounce him to the NKVD.

That evening as Misha helped his papa tidy a conference room in the Senate, there was some rare roast beef on the table, left over from a snack the catering staff had brought in while the generals and ministers worked on the latest strategy to stem the Nazi advance. Without a second thought, Misha wrapped it in a fresh white napkin and popped it in his pocket.

At lunchtime the following day, as they sat round the table with another lukewarm grey mince and potato dish, a furious row broke out between Nikolay and another boy in his class, Spartakus. In their previous lesson the politics tutor had been lecturing them on the achievements of the Soviet Union. Moscow's underground railway, he told them, was one of the great wonders of the world, and there was nothing like it in the capitalist countries.

Nikolay had said nothing during the lesson, but now

he was bursting to share his real thoughts. 'I read a railway book a few years ago that said London and Paris had underground railways built in the previous century. There were pictures, and everything, with tunnels and electric trains.'

'Capitalist propaganda,' huffed Spartakus. 'You are a class traitor, duped by imperialist jackals.'

Nikolay bristled. 'Well it was published by the People's Commissariat for Education. And as far as I know, they produce their books in the Soviet Union, and I don't think they are written by imperialists. Besides, these imperialist jackals are our allies now, aren't they?'

Spartakus was growing increasingly angry. 'No one has an underground system, apart from the Soviet Union. And the British imperialists might be our allies for the moment, but they will betray us as soon as it suits them.'

Barikada had come over and Misha wondered if he would join in. But he just sat there, his face a brooding scowl.

Misha tried to calm things down. 'Hey, never mind that. I've got something to share.' He pulled out the napkin and spread out the slices of beef on the table. If he'd got out a Fabergé egg, it would not have had a greater effect. Nikolay went to grab a piece. 'Hold on, I'll cut it up for us all,' said Misha.

He divided the beef into six more or less equal slices and passed them round so they could each take a piece. But when Misha got to Barikada the boy spat into the meat. Nikolay stood up and pushed him so hard he fell off his seat. 'Someone could have eaten that, you imbecile,' he shouted.

Barikada got to his feet and Nikolay stood up too, expecting to have to defend himself. But it was Misha Barikada turned on. Shaking with rage, he said, 'You think you're so special, don't you, Mikhail Petrov. You up there in the Kremlin with the rest of them who've betrayed us all. You with your fancy foods while we eat muck you wouldn't give to a dog. Well, enjoy it while you can. When the Nazis get here, they're going to nail you all to the Kremlin gates. And I'll be there to applaud.'

The cafeteria had come to a standstill. If Barikada had stripped himself naked and slashed his wrists, he could not have drawn more attention.

Barikada turned on his heels and walked out. The rest of them sat in stunned silence. No one said it, but they all knew they would never see Barikada again.

Valya had been teaching that afternoon and she and Misha walked back slowly to the Kremlin at the end of the day. It was still warm, with no hint of the autumn to come.

'I heard about Barikada,' said Valya.

Misha nodded.

'I wonder when they will come for him,' she said. 'Will they leave him a few days, or will they come at once?'

'Well, I won't inform on him,' said Misha. He was feeling a little nauseous now, knowing that he had done something that was going to contribute to the arrest of one of his schoolmates.

'It was stupid of him to talk like that so publicly. But people do stupid things when they're upset.'

'Maybe no one will say anything,' said Misha hopefully.

Valya looked at him and he knew she was about to say something crushing. 'Oh, Misha. Do you honestly think that no one in the entire canteen will go to the NKVD and tell them what happened? The Komsorg, the hall monitors, the canteen staff . . . the NKVD probably heard about it before the lunch break had ended.'

'But he didn't really do any harm, and he's not even eighteen.'

She looked at him with a twisted smile. 'Look at Beria. Look at Zhiglov. They are people who do not understand the meaning of mercy. The NKVD probably get paid or promoted by the number of arrests they make, the number of executions . . . the lower functionaries, obviously, I'm not talking about Beria, or Zhiglov here. I wouldn't want to be in Barikada's shoes.'

They had reached the great bridge across the Moskva and a slight wind was blowing off the water. Valya pulled her coat tight around her. 'You and I are luckier than most,' she said. 'We trust each other enough to talk. We know we will never betray each other to the NKVD.' She drew Misha closer and leaned her head on his shoulder. He longed to kiss her.

'Oh, Misha. I know it will never come to that. You are safe with me. I will never betray you.'

But that night, as he lay in bed, thinking about how it felt when she held him close, he realised that what also bound them was fear. It made him feel sad. Then he felt angry. Angry with this country that could make friends fear each other. He knew he would never deliberately betray Valya. But, though she might say she had no intention of betraying him, if they tortured Valya, Misha realised, she would say anything, eventually. And, in his heart, he knew he would too.

CHAPTER 16

End of September 1941

There was a knock at the door around nine in the evening. It sounded like Valya, which surprised Misha because she did not usually visit at that hour, unless she was coming with her father for a meal.

Sure enough, it was her.

'Guess what! I've received my call-up papers. I must report to Central Aerodrome at the start of December, and in the meantime I have to carry on teaching and stay fit and healthy.'

Misha hadn't seen her looking so happy for months – not since before the war. 'I think they will train me to fly the transport planes. Big ones like the Lisunov Li-2. That's the one they build under licence from the United States. I'll feel safe flying that. Unless I have to fly into battle with parachute troops. But that will be exciting. A story for my grandchildren . . . It's a marvellous aeroplane. Two Shvetsov nine-cylinder, air-cooled, radial engines, three hundred kilometres an hour, two thousand kilometre range . . . Misha! Pay attention!' She hit him on the shoulder. 'These things can fly from Moscow to London without stopping. Imagine that! And after the war I'll be all ready to be a civilian pilot.'

She could tell he was trying to stifle a yawn. 'I'll tell you a secret,' she continued. 'You know the hydroelectric dam on the Dnieper? The one that was the largest in Europe . . . the one that took ten years to build?'

Misha nodded. Every Soviet child had been told it was the greatest engineering achievement of the Soviet era. 'Well, they blew it up. *We* did it, to stop the Nazis getting it. Papa almost cried when he told me.'

Misha gasped. 'All the effort that went into building it, all that sacrifice, for nothing.'

She sat at the dining table and Misha made her a cup of tea. He got out the best bone china, the set they had been given when they first arrived at the Kremlin, which they'd been told had once belonged to Tsar Nicholas's cousin. Suddenly she seemed more serious.

'Misha, I also have bad news,' she said as she took her first sip of tea. 'The Germans are at Kiev. Isn't that where your brother works?'

Misha nodded. 'Papa thinks Viktor will join the partisans.'

'But if they're at Kiev they are heading down to Stalingrad. And the oilfields beyond. Leningrad is yet to fall. I keep hoping they have bitten off more than they can chew, but they keep pressing forward. And the weather is still mild. Maybe it'll be several weeks before the rain and the mud of the *Rasputitsa*. Who knows where they'll be by then? They already have the territory between Leningrad and Moscow – you can't get the train up there any more.'

'But what will happen if the Nazis get here?' asked Misha. 'Won't Comrade Stalin have to take the government cadres with him to the east?'

'I suppose. But it will be chaos, Misha. Everyone fleeing just as the winter starts to bite. It will be a catastrophe. They say the cruelty of the Hitlerites is breathtaking. In the conquered territories there are reports of mass shootings. Murder on a colossal scale. You know what they call us, don't you?'

Misha didn't.

'"*Untermensch*." That's a German word. It means subhuman.'

Misha laughed at that. It was almost too ridiculous.

'Do you think we will stop them?' he said. 'I always believed we had the greatest army in the world.'

'I used to think that too. But I don't think it matters

152

how good your soldiers are, if your generals are making the awful mess of it . . .'

There was a loud knock at the door. This was not the sort of knock a visiting neighbour would make. They both sat bolt upright and waited in silence. 'Don't answer. They might go away,' said Valya. 'Do you think your place is bugged? We've been saying things we shouldn't have.'

Misha picked up on her fear and began to feel very frightened himself. He realised they had not taken his papa's usual precaution of turning on the radio.

There was more knocking – louder and more persistent.

'I'll go. They know we are in, and the lights are on. They might take this as an admission of guilt.'

He went to open the door. Zhiglov was standing there, smoking a cigarette. His eyes lacked their usual focus and Misha could tell at once he was drunk. He reeked of alcohol.

'Young Comrade Petrov,' he said with mock familiarity, 'may I come in?'

Misha stood to the side and gestured for him to enter. He went to sit at the dining table where he stared for a moment at Valentina Golovkin. 'So this is why you took so long to answer the door,' he said with a sly grin.

He seemed confused. He opened his mouth to speak

and then stopped. Misha had never seen anyone in the NKVD behave like this. It made him immensely uneasy.

Then Zhiglov stood up, swaying slightly, and said, 'Petrov, I would like you to come to my apartment later tonight.' He looked at his watch. 'Around ten thirty? There is a matter I wish to discuss with you.'

With that, he turned on his heels and slammed the door behind him.

'What on earth was that about?' said Valya.

'I don't know,' Misha said. 'Will you come with me?'

She looked at him directly. 'Misha, you saw the way he looked at me. He's been cold with me since I saw him driving Beria's car. He quite transparently didn't ask me to come. I think you have to go alone. I could wait here until you get back, if you like? When do you think your papa will get home?'

'Sometime after midnight most likely,' Misha answered without looking at her.

'Don't be angry with me, Misha,' she said firmly. 'You know I can't come.'

'I'm not angry, Valya,' he lied. 'I'm just frightened.'

Valya went back home to leave a note for her father telling him where she was and returned to Misha's apartment just after ten. They sat at the dining table again, wondering what Zhiglov was going to say.

'Maybe he wants to recruit you to the NKVD?' said Valya.

'But my mother is an enemy of the people.'

'Foreign Secretary Molotov's wife is an enemy of the people. Chief Secretary Poskrebyshev's wife is an enemy of the people. Comrade Stalin's own son and his family are enemies of the people. There are so many enemies of the people it doesn't matter.'

When the Kremlin's Spasskaya Tower clock chimed the half-hour after ten, Misha took a deep breath and stood up. 'I will see you very soon, I hope,' he said.

She put a hand on his arm and squeezed. 'I'll wait until you get back.'

Misha took the short walk down the corridor to Zhiglov's apartment. He knocked quietly on the door, aware of the late hour. It was flung open. 'You are late,' said Zhiglov. He was nursing a cup of black coffee and his hair was wet from a bath or shower. Misha was amazed at the transformation from drunk to the seemingly sober figure that stood before him.

'Come and sit down,' said the Kapitan and beckoned Misha into a plush sitting room, with armchairs and a bright red leather sofa. Neither he nor Valya had ever been invited into the apartment when they used to collect Galina and Misha was surprised to see how bourgeois it was. Oil paintings adorned the walls. A beautiful marquetry cabinet stood in the space between two large windows. An intricate Persian carpet lay on the floor. It looked like a wealthy merchant's house from a painting in the pre-Revolutionary rooms at the State Tretyakov Gallery. Clearly, Kapitan Zhiglov knew some very well connected people.

Without asking, Zhiglov poured them both a large measure of vodka. 'To our health and happiness!' he said with a sardonic grin, knocking back his drink in a single mouthful. Misha shifted uncomfortably on the sofa, the fabric making an embarrassing squeak as he moved.

Misha took a sip of his vodka. He was no expert but even he could tell it was of the highest quality.

'Come on, knock it back,' scoffed Zhiglov. Misha did as he was told and coughed as the fiery liquid settled on his stomach. He placed his glass on the table and Zhiglov immediately filled it again.

'How is Galina getting on in Kuybyshev?' Misha asked.

Zhiglov ignored him. 'You know, my family come from the Ukraine,' he said.

Misha had guessed as much. Valya's father came from

the Ukraine and spoke in a similar accent. It was how they pronounced their 'r's that told you.

'I have heard terrible stories from my comrades in Kiev.'

Misha shuddered and wondered if Zhiglov had news of his brother.

'Tales of base treachery. The people greet the Nazis with salt and bread. They dress in their peasant finery and throw flowers at them. I've seen the photographs in the foreign magazines. I'm sure they aren't fakes.' He paused to light a cigarette. 'But I suppose we deserve it.'

Misha sat there flabbergasted and wondering what to say. Was this some kind of test? But Zhiglov obviously wasn't expecting a response.

'I was in Kiev during the worst of the famine,' he continued. 'You know about the famine?'

Misha shook his head.

Zhiglov wasn't convinced. 'Come on, Mikhail. Tonight we can be honest with each other.'

'I remember seeing a boy and girl at school when I was younger,' said Misha carefully, 'who had come from the west, probably from the Ukraine. They were very thin, sickly. They disappeared. We wondered if they had been too weak to live.'

'The ones who came to Moscow were lucky,' said

Zhiglov. 'Millions of them died. Those paintings you see in the galleries, photos in magazines of happy peasants on the collective farms celebrating the harvest . . . It's all just propaganda. In Kiev I saw bodies in the street every day, scores of them, flies buzzing around their eyes. People who had just dropped down dead from hunger. There was one time we were called out . . . Some peasant *muzhik* with his grimy beard and filthy grey overcoat and a tattered rope for a belt, there he was on the street, selling dismembered little children for meat, from a market stall.'

Misha felt sick.

Zhiglov filled his glass again.

'It was all deliberate of course – the famine, I mean,' he said. 'To punish the peasantry for their devotion to their god, and for their petty greed, and for their failure to support the Revolution. "Extermination by hunger", Beria called it. No wonder they welcomed the Nazis with open arms. And I would have done too, if I'd been one of them.'

Misha knew the Soviet leaders had made terrible mistakes, but he had never imagined they might be capable of such calculated wickedness.

'But it's got worse for them now. They've found out the Nazis are even crueller than we were. I heard this morning they've been rounding up the Jews, and there are a lot of Jews in Kiev. They've been killing them all –

tens of thousands shot in a couple of days in a ravine outside the city. And if they are doing that in the Ukraine, then I am sure they will be doing it everywhere else in Soviet territory they have captured. Galina's mother was Jewish. Does that make Galina a Jew? I think the Nazis would say so. Personally, although I know the *Vozhd* is wary of the Jewish people, *I* don't care. Some of our greatest revolutionaries were Jewish.'

Zhiglov poured another shot of vodka and downed it. 'But here's the thing. I thought the Nazis were better than that. I used to liaise with the German border forces in 1939, after the Molotov–Ribbentrop Pact. We used to dine together sometimes, us officers. They were good hearty fellows, those men. Decent in their own way. I thought I could work with them if they came – and we all knew they would one day. So I started to do some little things for them, passing on the odd titbit from Moscow. I let them know how unprepared we were. How easy it would be to overrun us. I dare say I wasn't the only one.'

Misha listened with growing horror. He went to sip his vodka and realised his glass was empty. Zhiglov filled it up. He looked at Misha with a steady eye. 'I've had enough of this,' he said. Misha didn't know whether he meant the vodka, the life he was leading or talking to him there that evening. An uneasy silence fell over the room.

'They'll put two and two together soon. I'll probably know the people who interrogate me. I've done it enough myself – beaten someone I used to have round for dinner. I hated that expression of relief they had when they saw it was me who had come to question them. No one lasts longer than a couple of weeks. We can get anyone to say anything. We can get them to admit their own mother is a German spy who's been sending state secrets to the Nazis for the last ten years, and dines out with Hitler and Göring every New Year's Eve. Everyone cracks because everything is permitted to us. And we have all the time in the world and they have nothing. Perhaps I should just tell them everything and save them the bother.'

Misha was struck dumb. Was this a trick to get him to say something he shouldn't? He just stared at the Kapitan, wondering what he would come out with next.

'I know what happened to your mother,' Zhiglov said out of the blue.

Misha sat bolt upright. A terrible fear squirmed in the pit of his stomach. 'Is she still alive?' he asked.

'I think she is,' Zhiglov replied with a small smile. 'They sent her to a camp called Noyabrsk. It's beyond the Ural Mountains. Way out in west Siberia. It's not too bad. Well, let me put it like this. There are plenty worse. She's working on a collective farm, if she's still alive. But

I have every reason to think she is. It's not a harsh regime. The political prisoners live in barracks outside the town.'

'Do you know why they arrested her?'

'Not my case, Mikhail.'

'Who denounced her?'

Zhiglov snapped, 'Don't push your luck.'

'Why are you telling me this?'

'You are a good boy,' said the Kapitan, smiling again. 'And Valentina is a decent girl. I was sorry when Beria took a shine to her. And Galina, especially, always liked you both.'

The Kapitan fell silent, then with a wave of his hand he said, 'You can go now.'

Misha walked unsteadily back to his apartment and stood outside the door. For a minute or two, he sat on his haunches there in the corridor, breathing deeply and trying to control his shaking limbs.

The apartment door opened. 'I thought I heard a noise outside,' said Valya. 'Are you all right?'

The vodka, and the awful tension and fear, welled up inside Misha and all at once he thought he was going to be sick. He dashed past her and reached the bathroom just in time.

She came and crouched beside the lavatory bowl, gently holding his hair away from his face.

When his nausea finally passed, she made him a pot of tea. Misha was grateful she had not asked him what had happened. He hadn't yet worked out how much he could safely tell her. As he sat sweating and willing himself not to be sick again, she placed a cup of tea on the table beside him and patted his arm.

'Tell me about it later, if you want to,' she said. 'Now, if you are not going to be sick again, I need to get to my bed.'

Misha wanted to stay up to tell his papa the news, but he felt too tired and too poorly. He dimly remembered hearing his papa arrive home in the early hours and sometime after that he was abruptly woken by a gunshot. He rushed out of his room to find Yegor standing in the living room, still in his work suit.

They both peered out of their front door and heard the sound of several footsteps running up the marble stairs.

'Quick, back inside,' said Yegor. 'Whatever has happened we don't want to get involved. And we definitely don't want to give anyone an excuse to think of us as suspects.'

The footsteps hurtled past their door very shortly afterwards. There were voices. Yegor recognised one of Zhiglov's neighbours protesting loudly. They heard banging and splintering.

'Back to bed,' said Yegor. Then, rather indignantly, he added, 'Misha, have you been drinking my vodka?'

'Papa, I went to see Kapitan Zhiglov. He told me Mama was alive. She's at a camp out in west Siberia – Noyabrsk, I think he said.'

Yegor hugged him tight. Misha could feel him breathing hard and suppressing a sob. 'Thank God. Thank God . . . But why did he tell you?'

'I don't know. He'd been drinking. And he kept giving me lots to drink too. I think that shot probably came from his apartment.'

Yegor hugged him again. 'Go back to bed now. We'll talk over breakfast.' Then, after a pause he said, 'I know of Noyabrsk. I prepared a report for the *Vozhd* on the factory relocations just last week. We have been rebuilding an aeroplane instruments factory there. Some of the politicals at the camp are going to work at the factory. Thank God she hasn't been working in a mine or digging a canal. That would probably have killed her.'

Then, just as he turned to go to bed, he said, 'Misha, the more we talk about Mama, the greater the danger to her and to us. For the moment we must not speak of it again.'

CHAPTER 17

The next afternoon Valya came round to see how he was. 'I thought I'd let you sleep off your hangover,' she said.

Then, when she could see Misha wasn't going to tell her, she said, 'I heard about Zhiglov. Papa came home for lunch and told me he'd been found with a bullet in his head. Papa thinks someone might have gone to his apartment and murdered him.'

Misha froze in horror.

'Don't worry, Misha, I didn't say anything. Are you sure no one saw you come or go last night?'

'It was late. No one was about.'

'Good. Then you should be safe.'

'But, Valya, my fingerprints are on one of the vodka glasses.'

'That's nothing. You could have been there that afternoon. The neighbours told what time they heard the gun go off. So they know it happened in the middle of the night.

'They say he had fallen foul of Beria,' she said, and then looked unsettled. 'Who hasn't?'

Papa came home at 7.00 p.m. that day. Early for him. Comrade Stalin had decided to carry on his work at the Kuntsevo *dacha* and instructed Yegor Petrov to go home to rest. Misha was pleased to have the opportunity to eat an evening meal with his father and Yegor said they would open an expensive bottle of French wine 'to celebrate their good news'. Yegor had picked up some frying steak from the Kremlin kitchens, although he said the chef there had told him he thought it might be horsemeat.

As they sat down to eat, Yegor poured the wine and raised his glass. Putting a finger to his lips he whispered, 'To Mama!'

They ate and drank heartily, and the bottle was soon empty. Misha hoped his papa wouldn't inflame his ulcer with all this rich food and drink.

'Misha, I want you to do me a favour,' said Yegor. 'I want you to go to our *dacha*. I want you to find something there and destroy it. Will you do that for me? I can't go myself. I'm too busy at work. And Comrade Stalin expects me to be only a phone call away, even when I am not in the office.'

Misha immediately felt anxious, but he had a strong suspicion this was about his mother and he was eager to do anything that would help him understand why she had disappeared. 'Of course, Papa.'

'You know how in the main room downstairs we have lots of paintings. Ones that you and Viktor and Elena did when you were younger, and ones that Mama did too, when she took her watercolours out in the garden. There's a big one of the poppies that bloom at the side of the garden. It was one of her best, so we put it in a big, expensive frame. Well, there's something inside that frame. Some documents and photographs that we should never have held on to, but your mama couldn't bring herself to throw them away. Now I know she's still alive I want to get rid of them. I think the Nazi soldiers might reach Meshkovo soon, and they will ransack the place, I'm sure of it. They are bound to smash things up, looking for loot.

'They'll be driven out, I'm sure of that too, and I don't want any of our soldiers or our policemen coming back and finding these photographs, especially the NKVD. Do you understand?'

'What do they show, Papa?' asked Misha.

'You'll see. But please put them in the stove and make sure they're all burned. You must go as soon as possible. I think it will be a nice day tomorrow. Make the most of the last of our warm autumn days and take a trip down there.'

CHAPTER 18

Early October 1941

The next day was a Rest Day and Misha had originally agreed to meet Valya and go to Gorky Park where some of their friends from school were gathering at the chess corner for a lunchtime picnic and a game.

When she came to bang on his door, he invited her down to the *dacha* on an impulse. He was sure his papa would consider this too great a risk but Misha trusted her absolutely.

She agreed at once and they set off with a small picnic. The metro was not running but after a brisk walk they reached Bryansk Station.

The carriage they sat down in was empty and remained so. Misha always enjoyed the slow journey down to Meshkovo. The train stopped at every little station en route and he would sit there with sunshine pouring through the windows enjoying the smell of smoke from the steam engine, and drink in the scents of the forest.

Before Mama was taken away, they would travel down for whole weekends. They would wind up the gramophone there and Mama and Papa would dance to one of Chopin's waltzes in the last light of the evening, while he and his brother and sister sat in the garden with their sketchbooks, pencils and crayons. He felt a deep yearning for those carefree days.

The further south-west they travelled from central Moscow, the greater his unease. Within weeks, maybe even days, anyone who had not fled Meshkovo would hear the grinding and clanking of tanks and then Nazi soldiers would appear out of the forest.

'So, how did you end up with this place? I thought your papa would want a *dacha* nearer the *Vozhd*,' said Valya, breaking into Misha's thoughts.

'No. He deliberately chose a place away from Kunt-sevo,' said Misha. 'I remember him talking about it over supper when I was younger. "I need to get away from the *Vozhd* sometimes," he said. I remember one time Mama said, "Even the most loyal servant needs time away from his master," and Papa flew into a rage. "Why do you have to belittle me like this?" he shouted.

'We were all there round the table, Viktor and Elena too. We didn't know where to look,' he confided. 'They argued a lot and often over little trivial things.'

'My parents used to bicker too, Mikhail,' said Valya. 'They all do it.' She looked out of the window. 'Sky looks good. I think it will be warm for the rest of the day.'

As the train trundled down through the industrial outskirts of Moscow and into the thick birch forests that surrounded the city, there were plenty of lunchtime picnickers setting up their little tables along the side of the rail track. It seemed strange to see such normality with such danger looming. The train passed a rotund *babushka* and her scrawny husband, quaffing a glass of red wine and puffing contentedly on their cigarettes, and Misha wondered if they had any idea what was coming.

'Surely they must have heard the news on the radio or read about it in *Pravda?*'

Valya agreed. 'It's plain enough. They said this morning our troops had fought a heroic defensive action at Mozhaysk. That's only a day or two away.'

'Hours if there's no one there to stop them,' said Misha glumly.

'Defeatist talk!' said Valya in mocking imitation of government radio announcements.

Misha leaned in and dropped his voice to barely a whisper. 'Valya, I have to tell you something.'

Valya flinched a little and moved away from him. Misha suddenly realised she thought he was going to tell her he loved her or something like that. He began to blush and quickly explained. 'It's about why I wanted to go to the *dacha*.'

'Go on,' she said warily.

'Mama left some photos hidden there. Photos that Papa doesn't want anyone to find. And some documents.'

Valya relaxed in an instant and began to laugh. 'Did she used to be a belly dancer or something?' she said.

Misha felt a little hurt at her flippancy. 'No. I don't know what they are. I just know where they are and that I have to burn them in the stove.'

'I'm sorry, Misha,' she said. She was looking embarrassed now. 'I thought you were going to say something else.'

She let that hang in the air. It was a conversation Misha definitely did not want to have.

The train arrived at Meshkovo shortly after noon. The day was at its hottest and when they reached the *dacha* Misha gathered a few twigs to add to the sticks in the little iron stove. Once he had started the fire and put a kettle on to boil, he asked Valya to help him take down the heavy gilt frame with his mother's watercolour of the poppies in the *dacha* garden.

'She was good, your mama,' said Valya. 'I wish I could paint like that. I wish I could paint at all!'

171

They laid the frame face down on the living-room table. The painting was held in place in the frame by a thin wood panel and tiny upholstery nails. Misha took a knife from the kitchen and began to gently prise the nails away.

Lifting the wooden panel off they immediately saw there was another underneath it and in the space between were several documents and three small photographs. Misha picked up the photos and quickly glanced through them. They showed a bewildering array of images.

There was a distinguished-looking naval officer with a beard, the white jacket of his uniform covered with medals, posing with a beautiful younger woman in a stylish black velvet dress and a fur hat with a feather in it. The couple had two small girls seated on their knees and both leaned against the other with cosy familiarity. The children were four or five and each wore an identical silk and lace dress. What puzzled Misha especially was how familiar these people seemed to him.

Valya was looking over his shoulder. 'Nice-looking bunch. Do you know who they are?'

There was another photograph of one of the girls, now aged about twelve or thirteen, posing by an elaborately decorated grand piano, one hand languidly placed on the keyboard, her shoulder covered by an ermine stole, a string of pearls around her neck.

'That looks a bit like your mama,' said Valya. Misha could see it too, but surely it couldn't be.

The final shot showed the two girls, now in their middle teens and wearing ball gowns, curtsying to a distinguished-looking man with a full beard and a uniform covered in braid and medals. Behind them was a table heaving with silverware, candelabras and china. The girls both looked the very picture of prosperous, happy young ladies. Behind them similarly well-dressed figures mingled and conversed. Perhaps it was a party, even a ball of some sort.

'Good God, Misha. That's the Tsar. That's Nicholas, with all his medals,' said Valya. 'Who are these people?'

Misha's hands began to shake. What had his mama been hiding here?

He looked at the documents. There were five of them in total, all from Moscow Imperial Conservatory, dated between 1911 and 1916. All declared that Anna Potemkin, of the Prince Alexander Baryatinsky Academy, had passed a succession of piano exams, each one with distinction.

'That can't be Mama,' said Misha. He sounded relieved. 'She could just about bash out "The Red Flag" and a few other communist songs.'

The kettle on the stove began to whistle. They sat on

the veranda in the watery sun enjoying a coffee and their little picnic.

'What are you going to do with this haul?' she asked.

'The piano certificates can go on the fire,' he said. 'I'm keeping the photographs.'

'Misha, I'm not going to nag you about this, but if your papa specifically asked you to destroy them, then shouldn't you do that?'

'Valya, it must be Mama in the photos. That's why Papa wanted me to burn everything.' All of a sudden he felt as though he had a cold stone in his stomach.

They sat in silence, then Misha took the piano certificates and tore them into pieces before throwing them into the stove. He put the three photographs in his top pocket and hammered the panel back into place in the gilt frame. Then, in a pleasant early afternoon haze, they wandered through the ragged silver birches of the forest, almost shoulder to shoulder, their feet kicking up the autumn leaves. Misha ached to touch her, even just hold her hand. Out of nowhere a cold wind blew down from the east and she shivered.

'Here, have my jacket,' he said, and had to hide his delight when she took it.

'It's my favourite time of year, the autumn,' she said wistfully. 'You savour every moment of a day like this, knowing it won't come again until May.'

'Time we headed back,' Misha said. 'There's a train just after four.'

Misha busied himself with the shutters and made sure the fire was out. 'I wonder if we'll ever come back,' he said.

He picked up the poppy painting, and she picked one of his pictures from the wall – something he had drawn with coloured pencils when he was ten or eleven, of the cat who used to visit their garden.

Weighed down with the frames, they hurried to the station. The train had still not appeared by twenty past four and both of them began to fret. Maybe the Germans had taken the line further down? But a few minutes later they heard a distant whistle and soon spotted the engine approaching with its plume of smoke.

Misha felt that familiar sinking feeling as the city began to close in around them. Factories, gas-storage cylinders and grain silos all stood black against the fading evening sky. Now an icy fear gripped him too.

'No air raids now, please God,' said Valya, which surprised Misha as he had never heard her mention God before in her life. She looked a little embarrassed. 'Wouldn't it be awful to be caught on a train in an air raid?' she said. 'The Hitlerites are strafing trains, even little local trains, not just the goods trains and the troop trains.'

Misha could picture it all too vividly. The Stukas with their screaming sirens, the roar of the engines, the stutter of machine guns, the splintering glass and wood, and an agonising death dancing to the steel whip of machine-gun fire.

But the sirens didn't sound and the train didn't even stop for an unexplained twenty minutes outside Leninsky Prospekt, like it usually did.

That evening as they walked over the bridge back to the Kremlin, weighed down with the paintings and a new secret, the cold wind continued to blow and the first few flakes of snow fell from the black sky.

CHAPTER 19

Misha sat up all evening waiting for his papa to come home. He had an awful squirming anxiety in the pit of his stomach and kept prevaricating about what he was going to do. Should he just go to bed and say nothing? Should he accuse his father of betraying his mother? After all, they had come for her but not him. What had that envelope full of money that he had found in the cupboard been for? Misha wasn't really sure how much he wanted to know about what had happened.

The Spasskaya Tower clock chimed through the quarter-hours. He tried to read but could not settle to anything. Eventually he began to doze. The door clicked and he woke with a start.

'Papa,' he called.

'Misha, you are still up. You have school tomorrow. Your mama would never have allowed this.'

Yegor Petrov came into the room. He was looking drawn. 'Did you to go Meshkovo?'

Misha nodded. 'Papa, I couldn't destroy those photos. I have brought them back. They're of Mama, aren't they?'

Yegor just nodded. In his mind Misha had been through the scene many times and he had imagined his papa shouting or even hitting him. He never expected this. His papa took the photos from him. 'I will burn them,' he said softly. 'You know what would happen if anyone found them.'

Yegor sat down on the sofa and rubbed his tired eyes. Then he went to the drinks cupboard and pulled out a bottle of vodka and poured himself a shot.

He drank it in a single gulp and then poured another. Misha waited uneasily.

'You should know the truth, I suppose,' said Yegor.

He took a further slug of vodka and beckoned for Misha to sit beside him.

He turned on the radio and as one of Tchaikovsky's concertos played quietly in the background he began. He spoke in the kind of cautious voice people used when they talked about forbidden things in cafes and parks.

'Mama has an interesting history. One that the Party would not approve of. When Zhiglov said she is still alive, I didn't want anyone to find out any more about her than

178

they already know. They might want to punish her even more. That is why I sent you to destroy those things.'

'Your mother was born into a noble household, Misha. Imagine. She was one of them! Don't look so shocked. It's not that bad. She wasn't a countess or a princess or anything. Her mother – your *babushka*, who you never knew – was one of the servants. She had an affair with the Count in his Moscow mansion. He was a navy officer. Look, that's him in the photograph with her.

'He didn't cast her out when he discovered her condition. Indeed he made sure your grandmother and her baby were well looked after with a nice apartment in Arbatskaya and a monthly income. He used to visit your grandmother frequently when your mother was tiny. Not long after, Aunt Mila was born. There they are in the photo with their father and mother. He took an interest in them both. Anna had letters from him telling her she and Mila were the most beautiful girls in Russia, and that he would always be there to look after them. She used to keep the letters with the photographs and piano certificates. But Mama always worried about these things. The letters were the most obviously incriminating evidence so they had to go in the stove. How she cried when she had to do that.

'The Count paid the fees for them to be sent to a good

school. They made up a story about their father being killed during the Russo-Japanese War. He paid for piano lessons too. Look at her there at the piano. She was a beautiful young woman, wasn't she? I can't tell you how much Anna missed being able to play. I only heard her once – when we were staying at a hotel on our honeymoon. She played exquisitely – Mozart, Chopin, Beethoven, all from memory. But that was a reckless thing to do. This was in 1920. There were people giving her funny looks and whispering. It taught her to keep quiet about her ability. For a woman her age, it was too much of a clue that she had had a bourgeois upbringing. Now, with music schools for talented proletarians, it's OK, but those sorts of accomplishments in a woman of your mother's generation made you very suspect. You were probably a non-toiling element, a class enemy.

'She told me about her background before we married. Of course I was shocked but I wasn't going to betray her. Her father, the Count, was an interesting man, to be sure. You know, he was an officer aboard the battleship *Potemkin* – one of the officers who sided with the mutineers during the 1905 revolution. Your mother borrowed that name for herself. He was sent to Siberia by the Tsar for his pains, where he lived in a grand house with his servants. Not the sort of exile you'd expect these days, where you count yourself lucky to be sent to a work camp rather than a mine.

'Well, he came back eight years later, just before the war began in 1914, and even though he had tuberculosis, which he'd caught in exile, he went to fight the Germans. He survived the war and he joined the Whites in the Civil War. Mama had lost touch with him during the war but her mother told her just before she died that she thought he was killed fighting the Revolutionary Guards at Tsaritsyn. I might have even fought against him myself.'

Misha was beginning to feel really upset. 'But it's not Mama's fault her father was an aristocrat,' he said. 'Didn't Comrade Stalin himself say you can't punish the children for the sins of their parents?'

'Misha, you are old enough to know that what people say and what they do is sometimes quite different. Look what happens to the families of the soldiers who surrender to the Nazis. When Yakov, the *Vozhd*'s own son for Christ's sake, was captured this summer, even his wife Yulia and their two children were arrested and sent to prison. So close relatives of aristocrats who fought for the Whites – like your mama and you – they would be the lowest of the low. Come on, you have seen enough of your fellow students being unmasked to know this.'

Misha sat there boiling with anger. His mother was

everything a good communist should be. She was totally dedicated to her students. She had been his inspiration when he volunteered to teach the factory workers. There was nothing snobby about her, like those sad old matrons you saw with their china cups and black lace dresses, having furtive conversations in cafes. Mama was everything that a new Russian should be. Her life, her political consciousness, had been 'remoulded' by the Soviet Union. But evidently that was not enough to save her from the NKVD.

'This country has gone rotten from the inside,' said Misha softly. 'Papa, how can you continue to serve a man who is responsible for the very worst of it?'

Yegor snapped. 'We do what we do to keep alive, and keep our family alive.'

Misha waited for him to calm down.

'Why did you never tell me what you knew about Mama?' asked Misha.

His father took Misha by the hand – something he had not done since he was ten or eleven. 'Misha, children who have noble blood are pariahs. They are not allowed to go to university. You were always the brightest of our children. Wouldn't it have been terrible if you had had to leave school because Mama had noble blood? The less anyone knew, the safer you would be.'

Misha could barely contain his disgust. 'What a stupid waste,' he said. 'What a ridiculous waste of people's talents. The children of these people don't deserve punishment, any more than the wives and children of soldiers who have been captured.'

All at once, that familiar look of stark terror returned to Yegor's face. 'Misha, never, never talk like that, not even to your own papa,' he whispered. 'You may be young but they will take you away and you'll be shot if anyone hears you saying such things.'

It was then that Misha realised his papa was as terrified of Stalin and Beria as everyone else. A man who could imprison his own son's wife and children would think nothing of ordering the liquidation of an old comrade.

'So what do you know about Mama's arrest?' asked Misha. 'Why did they take her and not you? I still don't understand why she was arrested. Was it her background?'

'No, it wasn't that. Mama said things . . .'

'What things? Who to?'

'To the *Vozhd*. She picked her friends unwisely. I will tell you. Swear you will never repeat it . . . When we first came to live here, Mama made friends with a couple, the Usatovs.'

Misha remembered them. They were the couple who introduced the Petrovs to fine wine. The husband,

Grigory, was a naval attaché at the Kremlin. Misha could picture him clearly in his uniform. There weren't many navy people at the Kremlin and Grigory really stood out. Vera always arrived with presents – usually a book for Viktor and Elena and some chocolate from the foreign provisions shop for Misha. Vera and his mama would sit and chat for hours over coffee.

'They were not a good choice for friends. In early 1940 Grigory was arrested as a Trotskyite spy and two weeks later the NKVD came for Vera too. Your mama was convinced she was entirely innocent. She told me Vera was a dedicated communist to her soul. So Anna went to plead with the *Vozhd* to let her go. Mama knew Comrade Stalin liked her. But she pushed her luck too far. I think he thought she had come to seduce him when she asked to speak to him in private. She told me he was very frosty with her when he realised why she wanted to be alone with him. As soon as she told me what she had done, I knew it was only a matter of time before they came for her. I thought they would come for me too. I was surprised when they only took her.'

'Why didn't you try to save her? ' asked Misha, trying to keep the anger from his voice. 'You were Stalin's old comrade. Didn't you save his life? Surely he must listen to some people . . .'

Yegor Petrov sat up very straight. Misha could see a blood vessel bulging in his bald head.

'Misha, your mama was arrested for trying to save someone she cared about. I couldn't risk leaving you on your own. Who would have cared for you?

'I did manage to do something for her. Just after I discovered she had been arrested I paid three thousand roubles to one of Zhiglov's comrades in the NKVD to get her sent to a work camp that wasn't going to be the death of her. I heard nothing more about it. Zhiglov's contact disappeared not long afterwards, so I never knew if she was sent to an easier camp. In fact, I never knew until the other night whether or not they had just shot her. But maybe that is the best three thousand roubles I ever spent.'

The envelope of money. Misha felt an overwhelming relief, mixed with shame for ever having suspected his father.

Yegor spoke again, his own sadness tinged with anger. 'Your mama should have known better. I witnessed several people trying to intervene on behalf of a friend or relation. You know what happened? Nothing – if they were lucky. But plenty weren't. Morozov's wife, remember her? She tried to get the *Vozhd* to release her brother. Dressed up in her best cocktail frock, flirted with him all night . . .'

He pulled a finger across his throat.

'And that fool Leonov, who I used to work with, addressed the *Vozhd* as Iosif Vissarionovich. Stalin hates overfamiliarity. He came out of that meeting shaking like a leaf. Disappeared a week later. I wasn't going to jeopardise my life and your future on a fool's errand. Look at me, Mikhail.' His voice was trembling. 'Look at me.'

Misha met his father's intense gaze.

'You would have been put in a children's home. Or you might have been arrested along with me. They would have sent you to a penal battalion, Mikhail. You would have been slaughtered by the Nazis when the war broke out . . .'

Misha realised, like never before, how fortunate he had been to have his father to protect him.

'I have survived for five years in this snake pit. And I have provided a good life for you. Hardly anyone in the country lives better than us. And until your mother went we were all happy.'

Misha was blushing with shame and staring at his feet.

Yegor began to speak very quietly. 'I have seen it all. The Party elders who tried to convince Stalin to slow down, the ones who tried to stop the famine in Ukraine, the ones who thought we had come too far too quickly . . . good communist men and women, who had given their whole lives to the Soviet cause. They all thought they had the stature and authority to speak openly, in the spirit of communist brotherhood. They all went. All of them shot in a squalid basement somewhere, begging for forgiveness sometimes. Yes, I heard reports of their executions. I think he let me listen deliberately, to remind me to stay in line. We have created a monster, Mikhail. I am the monster's servant and I know the rules. Which is why you and I are still alive. Did you ever stop and think who lived in this apartment before us? I heard stories . . . I'm surprised they don't come to haunt us.

'All of us in that office know what it feels like to lie in our bed, listening to the knocking on doors and praying it would be your neighbour and not you. The scuffles on the stairs, the screaming children as their parents were manhandled away. I spend my life trying to prevent that happening to you and me. I don't even know what they charged your mother with. Something utterly ridiculous. "Spying for the Germans. A factory saboteur, a wrecker. An enemy of the people . . ." Complete fantasy. Alice in Wonderland.

'I heard of men who had raised up factories from bare fields, tortured into admitting they deliberately sabotaged their own machinery. Men who had built great steel works . . . tortured until they confessed to throwing artillery shells into their own blast furnaces. Bizarre crimes, not even barely plausible. Insane.'

'But, Papa, we hear about the Trotskyite wreckers and imperialist spies almost every day at school. Surely some of it must be true?'

'Most of it is a fairy tale, Mikhail. Was your mother a wrecker? Was she a Nazi spy? She's no different to the others. They were just more important. More known to the people. We have failed the people. The Revolution has gone sour.

'My son, I want you to understand why things are as they are. I want you to survive.'

CHAPTER 20

The next morning Misha left the apartment to be greeted by an oppressive grey sky and biting northerly wind. There was no snow but he could taste the chilly moisture in the air and hoped the downpour would hold off until he reached his school.

The news on the radio had been bad. There was no talk of any victories or advances, or the Hitlerites being driven back, only 'heroic defenders'. And the towns and cities the radio announcer mentioned were getting closer to Moscow by the day.

As he walked through Cathedral Square, a strange smell crept into his nostrils. The nearer he got to the Borovitskaya Tower, the stronger it became. It was the sort of unsettling odour you noticed in a really cheap second-hand clothes shop or market stall – a dense fug of unwashed clothing and unwashed bodies.

As Misha walked through the tower gates and out on

to the bridge, he was confronted by an extraordinary sight. The street was clogged with a great swathe of exhausted, filthy people. There were old men with straggly beards, *babushkas* of all shapes and sizes, and wan little children, blank faces staring into nothing. Misha realised at once they were fleeing from the approaching Nazi army.

Some of the crowd carried their possessions in hand-carts, others looked as if they were wearing all the clothes they owned. Most had their heads covered in scarves or blankets. A lucky few had an emaciated donkey or horse, to drag a cart stuffed with tottering belongings.

What unnerved Misha was their utter silence. There was the clop of hooves, the trundle of wheels, and the shuffling of thousands of feet, but clearly no one here had energy to waste in conversation. They exuded a misery that was almost palpable.

He heard the honking of geese and instinctively looked to the empty sky, then realised the geese were there among the crowd, close by him, being driven in a small flock by a little boy with a stick. Their honking set off other farm animals among this ragged procession. Cattle began to low and sheep bleated pitifully.

Here and there uniformed men and women directed the flow, and as Misha looked over Lebyazhi Lane up to

Ulitsa Mokhovaya he could see no end to this stream of people. The Militia and the army personnel were hardly needed to keep order, they were just there to direct them wherever they were going. Everyone seemed too worn out to be angry or violent. Misha guessed they would be heading for the Highway of the Enthusiasts, the road east out of Moscow to the distant Ural Mountains and Siberia. He wondered when these people had last eaten and guessed they must be starving.

He ran immediately to his apartment and raided the refrigerator and pantry, coming back laden with a canvas bag filled with bread, dried meat and apples. Standing at the edge of the crowd he handed out his provisions to whoever he thought looked most in need. At first his offerings were snatched away with barely a word but then, as the crowd began to realise what was happening, there was a mad scramble that knocked him flat on to the cobblestones and saw his bag and its contents spilled on to the floor, and the remains of the food snatched away. It reminded him of the time his family were set on by a flock of gulls when they had laid out a picnic on the banks of the Dnieper.

Misha had cut his hand in falling and he hurried again to his apartment to wash the dirt away. As he ran his hands under the bathroom tap, the Spasskaya Tower on

191

the north-east wall of the Kremlin struck one o'clock and he realised with mounting anxiety that he was going to be late for school.

He took a route through the back streets to avoid the great stream of people and passed several small factories and workshops that were bustling with activity. As he glanced through windows and open warehouse doors, he could see men and women dismantling machinery and packing whatever they could into crates and boxes. It seemed like the whole of Moscow was getting ready to flee.

For a single selfish moment, Misha regretted being so generous with his food supply. He had taken it for granted that he and Papa would always have enough food in the Kremlin.

The meals they were getting in school had become even more frugal – and so bad he was grateful for the small portions. He sometimes brought a picnic with him these days but Misha had not brought food to share since the incident with Barikada. He ate his own provisions quickly and surreptitiously, when he was alone in a classroom, preparing to teach the younger ones. He did not want anyone to see him and make him feel like a greedy noble stuffing his face while peasants starved around him.

Today he arrived to find his class of twelve-year-olds half empty. 'Where are the others?' he asked the fifteen or so children that clustered around the desks at the front.

'Please, Comrade Petrov,' said a tall girl with plaits and a grubby beige smock, 'we had a terrible time getting here through the crowds. Maybe the rest have given up trying and gone home?'

'I had trouble too,' said Misha. 'Well done for making an effort to get here. You should be proud of yourselves.'

'Please, comrade,' said one small boy. 'I only live in the next street.'

They all giggled at that and Misha let himself smile too. 'Well, you can't be proud but the rest of you can.'

'Comrade, who are the people out in the street?' asked another child.

Misha didn't want to tell them they were fleeing from the Nazis. It would alarm them terribly. 'They are being moved by our brave soldiers, so they don't get hurt in the fighting,' he said, then quickly changed the subject. 'So, who has read the passage which I set you for homework?'

All of the children raised their hands and Misha felt really pleased. Despite it all, he enjoyed teaching the younger classes. Once he had adjusted to what these children were actually interested in, he had discovered they responded well to him, and he had little trouble keeping order, even with the rowdier children. It was all down to confidence, he decided. Make it look like you know what you're doing and they will respond, and behave.

But as Misha was reading another passage from *War and Peace*, he noticed something at the back of the class that filled him with horror. All Soviet classrooms had a poster or painting of Comrade Stalin on their walls and this one had too – surrounded with drawings the children had done of the May Day military parades.

Someone had drawn a great dagger through Stalin's head, from one ear to the other, the point dripping blood. Two vampiric fangs jutted from his lips, and blood trickled down his chin. A childish hand had scrawled УБИЙЦА – Murderer – on the *Vozhd*'s forehead. Above, curving around the white space that surrounded his head, was written УБЛЮДОК – Bastard.

Misha stopped reading. He had never seen anything like this before. He wondered immediately whether he should carry on and pretend he had not seen it, but the children noticed his shock and while some turned round to follow the direction of his gaze, others began to snigger. They had noticed already.

All at once the class was in uproar. 'Please be quiet,' Misha pleaded. He had decided on a plan.

'Class, settle down.' His voice was harsher. And this

time they responded. Misha did not want any of the remaining teachers, or the Komsorg, coming to see what the trouble was.

'Does anyone know who did this?' he asked in a gentle matter-of-fact voice.

He looked at the children's faces. No one was giving anything away.

Misha walked over to the poster and reached up to take it down. He rolled it carefully into a tube and placed it beneath his desk. 'Now where were we?' He smiled, and continued teaching as if nothing had happened.

Afterwards, when the children had filed out to another lesson, Misha locked the classroom door. With trembling hands he tore the poster into small pieces and hid it in his knapsack. He was not going to report the incident. He did not want an inquisition, with the Komsorg trying to find heretics like Torquemada or the Witch-finder General. These children had enough on their plate waiting for the Nazis to arrive.

That evening Misha sat alone in his apartment, scouring the latest edition of *Pravda* for clues on the progress of the war. He saw, with a sickening feeling in his chest, a news piece on Nazi atrocities in the Smolensk area. A camera had been found on the body of a German soldier and the film inside it told a grisly story. Two partisans had been captured and hanged. A series of shots reproduced in the paper told the story in graphic detail. There was a teenage girl, maybe his own age, proud but bruised, surrounded by jeering German soldiers, her hands tied behind her back. She was wearing the same sort of stripy pullover Yelena often wore at school, and had a placard around her neck, saying *I AM A TERRORIST*, written in Russian. Misha could barely bring himself to look further. He glimpsed another shot of two dangling figures, then folded the paper over so he could not see the photographs, and read the article.

The brave partisan girl's final words of defiance to the Hitlerites were: 'You cannot kill all 169 million of us.' With such unquestionable revolutionary spirit, how can we lose the war!

Yelena, he knew, faced exactly the same fate. Only blind chance, or extraordinary luck, would save her from the noose or a German bullet. He put the paper down and sobbed until he had no more tears.

CHAPTER 21

Mid-October 1941

Over the previous week the weather had turned the ground slushy – but now it was icy cold. Nikolay had told him slushy was good. Mud made it difficult for an army to advance. But colder weather meant firmer ground. The colder it got the easier it would be for the Nazi tanks to press forward and break through to the city. They were only a whisker away now. Out on the street, he would see people anxiously scanning the skies. There had been talk of German parachutists landing in their thousands and whenever a squadron of aircraft flew overhead citizens would stop in their tracks, expecting to see a stream of tiny figures emerge from them. Only when the planes had flown by would they move on.

The vast processions of displaced peasants and civilians fleeing the western front line had slowed now, but the streets were still clogged with refugees, easily recognisable by their shabby suitcases and exhausted expressions. Misha had got used to navigating his way around the small herds of sheep or pigs that sometimes accompanied them.

These days he often wondered if he was wasting his time making the journey to school, especially as there were so few teachers and children turning up. School had become a great rumour mill where the latest scare stories spread fear like a contagious disease. Many of the children travelled to school by the tram and metro and both were becoming increasingly unreliable. Whenever they stopped running, people would say the Nazis had reached the outlying stops. When Misha saw a lone tram on Ulitsa Gertsena one day, he half expected it to be full of German soldiers.

Even the most sensible people would tell the most outlandish stories. Now, after a couple of weeks of such rumours, Misha was almost starting to believe them. As he arrived at school, Nikolay ran up to greet him with the news that Nazi soldiers had been sighted at the metro terminus at Sokol – just to the north-west of the city centre.

'Nikolay, you have lost your mind!' Misha said. 'If they were that close, we would have heard the fighting. You know, rifles, machine guns, artillery shells.'

Nikolay looked crestfallen. 'Well. Sergey told me his

own father had seen German tanks on the other side of Zoo Park. He said he could see the muzzle flashes from their guns.'

Misha felt disappointed. These were the sort of stories his eleven- or twelve-year-olds would tell him in class.

'I listened to the news before I came out and it said there was still fierce fighting around Mozhaisk,' he replied. 'That's still a hundred kilometres away.'

Nikolay scoffed. He lowered his voice and said, 'Misha, you don't still believe what the radio tells you, do you?'

Misha felt angry. 'Nikolay, I'm not an idiot. If I hear the words "heroic defensive actions", I know that's probably where the fighting is.' He tried hard not to lose his temper and put a hand on his friend's shoulder. 'When we start to hear the artillery, that's when we need to get worried.'

But a hundred kilometres was nothing. You could drive it in an hour. And there was danger within the city walls too. There had been a strict blackout since the summer, when the Nazis had captured airbases in range of the capital. Tales of rape and looting were rife and he and Valya always walked home together at the end of the day. The previous Day Four they had seen a small crowd smash a grocery shop window on Ulitsa Serafimovicha. Misha walked past it the next day and saw the looters had tried to set it alight. Fortunately for the other shops and apartments in the block, the fire didn't take.

Much as he disliked the Militia men, who were usually such a visible and menacing presence, he missed them now. Misha hadn't seen a policeman or a squad of soldiers out on the street for several days, although the Kremlin seemed to be full of them. Maybe the *Vozhd* was afraid of an uprising and thought most of Central Moscow's police and soldiers were needed to protect him.

There were so few teachers and pupils that day that school finished early and Misha returned home to find the Kremlin buzzing with activity. Tanks guarded all the main entrances and scores of trucks were parked up inside the walls. Clearly something significant was happening.

He entered his apartment to find his father packing a suitcase.

'I am so glad you are home. Hurry and pack as much as you can carry,' said his papa. 'The *Vozhd* has decided to leave Moscow. Essential staff and their families are travelling out tonight.'

'Where are we going?' asked Misha.

'You'll find out soon enough. It's three days on a train, I would guess. So we must bring provisions too.'

'What about the Golovkins?' asked Misha. 'Is Valya coming?'

Yegor snapped. 'Anatoly Golovkin is staying here. He volunteered. We need to keep a skeleton staff at the Kremlin. Moscow will not surrender without a fight.'

'I must go to say goodbye.'

'You'll do no such thing. Misha, we have to be at Kazan Station in the next hour or so. The Hitlerites have broken through on all three main highways to the west. There are trucks waiting already in the Ivan Square for us and our suitcases. I don't want to leave you behind.'

Misha went to his room and filled his suitcase with as much as he could carry. At first he was angry because Papa wouldn't let him go to the Golovkins, then he felt tearful because he was leaving his home and his life and his friends.

To Misha, leaving the apartment seemed unreal, like a dream he was having. As his papa locked the door, it occurred to him that he might never see his home again. He had an image in his mind of Mama in her green evening gown, about to go out to a Kremlin banquet with Papa. Tears welled up, and he quickly distracted himself by grabbing his heavy case and marching down the corridor.

'Hey, Misha,' Papa called. 'You have to carry some

food too.' He gave him a knapsack stuffed with bread, dried meat and jars of pickled vegetables.

They walked out into a chill evening drizzle and hauled their heavy cases to Ivan Square. In the blackout this was a dangerous place to be. Lorries were already leaving, carefully weaving through milling hordes of people, their headlights muffled to a dim glow. The Petrovs were quickly consigned to an open-backed canvas-covered truck. Yegor recognised several of his colleagues and their families and greeted them briskly but these were people Misha did not know and he wished again that the Golovkins were coming.

As most of the passengers in this truck were women and children, Misha thought it would be polite to sit nearest the exit, and he watched his world disappear as the truck drove past the looming shadows of the cathedrals. He peered through the gloom hoping for a last glimpse of Valya, thinking she might have heard about them leaving and come out to wave the trucks off, but he couldn't see her anywhere. When they drove through the Borovitskaya Tower and turned north, he realised he would probably never see her again.

Misha had not pressed his papa on where they were going. In fact, he half wondered if they would be making the whole journey by truck. He imagined it would be somewhere east of the Ural Mountains, like Kuibyshev, where Stalin's daughter Svetlana had spent the early weeks of the war. That was a good thousand kilometres away and the thought of travelling there in the back of the truck filled him with dismay. He began to give himself a pep talk. He would try to think positive thoughts. He was going somewhere pleasant and almost certainly warmer than Moscow. And he would be out of range of the German bombers, and certainly away from the terrible danger of the street fighting that was sure to break out when the Germans reached Moscow.

The truck drove past all the familiar landscapes, now just dim silhouettes in the blackout: Red Square, the Bolshoi Theatre and the Lubyanka. A strong smell of burning hung in the damp air, most noticeably as they passed government buildings. Misha guessed they were disposing of documents and occasionally he caught a glimpse of a bonfire in a courtyard or sparks rising into the air. That was strictly against blackout regulations and would normally render its perpetrators liable to the most severe accusations. They had told him at his *Komsomol* air-raid training that traitors and saboteurs would be lighting fires to guide the German bombers to important targets.

The convoy swung north-west up the long stretch of Ulitsa Myasnitskaya. Misha began to hope they were heading for the cluster of railway stations on Komsomol-skaya Square.

Ordinarily, such a journey would take ten or fifteen minutes from the Kremlin at this time of night, but that evening progress was slow. Traffic was particularly heavy. Misha had never seen so many cars on the road at once. Most were bursting with luggage both inside and strapped precariously to the roof, and Misha glimpsed anxious faces through their windows. Large trucks, loaded with factory machinery, were also caught in this human tide, and thousands of people were heading out on foot, dragging bags and cases with them. These weren't the peasants Misha had seen earlier in the month, fleeing from the Germans with their livestock; these were citizens of Moscow.

Through the gloom and drizzle, Misha could see smashed shop windows and figures emerging clutching table lights, chairs, typewriters – a mad assortment of anything they could find. He wondered if there was any food left to loot, or bottles of vodka, or whether these had all gone days ago.

From somewhere ahead they heard gunfire, and everyone around him stiffened. The truck, already moving at barely walking speed, came to a halt. Misha stood up and peered cautiously around the side of the canvas cover.

People looked terrified and the crowds on the streets were hurrying away from the sound. Misha heard people shouting, 'The Germans are here.'

There was more shouting and more gunfire. Misha had his *Komsomol* membership card in his jacket top pocket. If the Hitlerites searched him and found it, he would be shot on the spot. He wondered if he could take it out and throw it away without anyone noticing. Some-one might see and denounce him for defeatism and cowardice in the face of the enemy. And if he was stopped by Soviet soldiers or Militia men and he didn't have it, he would be in all sorts of trouble. They might even shoot him as a spy or a deserter.

Ahead in their convoy, he could see fighting had broken out in one of the trucks. Soldiers were rushing towards the trouble and Misha felt an odd sort of relief. Whatever was happening was between Russians and Russians. The Germans were not here after all. He imme-diately sat down on his suitcase again. He didn't want to see people being shot. No one asked him what was happening. His fellow passengers were sitting back, their faces stiff with fear, not even daring to see what was going on in the street.

Then Misha started to worry that people in the crowd might try to board their truck.

There was more shouting, but no gunfire. After a further delay, the truck lurched forward. Everyone sat back now, their faces in the shadows.

Ten minutes later, after much stopping and starting and honking of horns, the truck drove under a gateway, through a dense phalanx of soldiers carrying rifles with fixed bayonets, and under the cover of a vast iron canopy. Misha recognised the interior of Kazan Station at once. That gave him a clue about where they were going. It was from here that trains departed for the east: to Kazan, Yekaterinburg, Ryazan and Kazakhstan.

Soldiers appeared and helped them down, taking suitcases to load on to trolleys. 'Comrades, you are to board the train on platform six,' said an officer. 'We will load your cases, so take what you need for the journey. Carriages three to seven have been reserved for government administrators and their families.'

The convoy of trucks had parked inside the enormous concourse of the station, which was almost deserted, apart from a few squads of soldiers, and a scattering of travellers, sitting despondently on their luggage. Misha coughed as exhaust from the truck caught in his throat. He peered through the gloomy electrical light of the station interior. He could see piles of abandoned bags, cases and blankets covering the entire marble floor, vast as a football pitch.

The whiff of smoke from the locomotives also caught in his nostils. That was reassuring. There were trains and they were running. The new arrivals were hurried through to the platform. The train before them seemed to go on forever. He guessed there must be thirty passenger and goods carriages at least. The platforms were not covered and Misha and his father were damp with drizzly rain by the time they reached the forward section of the train. The compartments were packed solid with passengers who had arrived earlier and by the time they got to carriage number three Misha was beginning to worry that they would not be able to find a place to sit.

'Quick, Misha, two seats at the far end,' said Papa.

They were lucky. Within a couple of minutes the rest of the carriage had filled to capacity. Two thickset middle-aged men in civilian clothes sat opposite them. They nodded a greeting but looked too intimidating to engage in conversation. Misha immediately assumed they were NKVD, there to listen for seditious conversations. He thought they would have been better off sending two young women in floral dresses, or a couple of lanky book-ish types. These men were too obvious.

'Comfortable?' asked Papa. Misha nodded. He could imagine sleeping in a plush velvet seat like this. He hoped he would not have to give his place up for an old lady or a mother with a baby. That would mean three days standing up or sleeping on the floor.

Misha noticed how the carriage now smelled faintly of damp coats from the rain and thought it was funny how different these passengers were from the average bunch on a Moscow train or tram. On a night like this the smell of fusty damp clothing in an overcrowded tram would be almost unbearable.

The flow of passengers milling outside the window ceased. The platform was now deserted except for a handful of soldiers pacing up and down with their rifles. These did not have their bayonets attached, which was reassuring. Misha could see his papa getting more fidgety by the minute. Whistles blew, there were shouts, but it was always other trains that left the station rather than theirs.

'We must hope there are no air raids tonight,' said Yegor, and Misha remembered again his story about being caught on a train by fighter aircraft during the Civil War.

'We must guard against defeatist talk, comrade,' said one of the men sitting opposite.

As if to taunt his papa, the wail of the air-raid siren began to rise and fall only moments later. Some of the passengers got up and headed for the exits, but the soldiers standing by the doors told them to return to their seats.

An awful silence descended on the carriage. A few seats down, a baby began to wail, impervious to the pleas of its mother. Eventually the crying subsided to a whimper and everyone sat there listening for the drone of engines and the *crump* of bombs. Gazing into the sky, Misha could see the usual searchlight fingers but there were no bursts of anti-aircraft fire. Shortly after they all heard bombs exploding and the baby began to cry again. But the bombs were some distance away and they did not appear to be getting closer.

They waited another anxious hour, until the monotonous drone of the all-clear siren sounded across the city. At once the train began to shudder and vibrate as the locomotive began to make steam. But still the train didn't move.

Yegor's patience broke. 'Misha, go to the door and lower the window. Try to see what is happening.'

Misha half expected the two men opposite him to warn them against undermining the Soviet war effort by spreading alarm and unease, but they seemed as keen as anyone to know what was going on. He only had to squeeze past a few people to get to the door. He couldn't see any soldiers out on the platform so he opened the window just enough to poke his head out and peered up to the front of the train.

The clouds had thinned and the drizzle had stopped. Moonlight now illuminated the rooftops and spires around the station. He could see the locomotive well enough on the curve of the platform, its giant wheels cloaked with steam. There, close to the engine driver's compartment, half hidden by the billowing steam, a familiar figure paced up and down. His hands were deep in his pockets, an unlit pipe in his mouth. The *Vozhd*.

Misha felt relieved to see him, assuming they were definitely about to go now that Stalin was there at the front of the train. But as he watched, he saw the *Vozhd* beckon to a colleague inside the first carriage. Another figure emerged and the two stood close in conversation. Stalin was shaking his head. The other man was nodding. This did not look good.

A sudden shout gave Misha such a shock he recoiled and hit his head on the top of the window. 'Get back inside,' said one of the guards on the platform. Then he instructed everyone to draw the blinds on their carriage windows.

'Maybe there is bomb damage on the line ahead,' said Papa.

As they waited, Papa gave Misha a few slices of salami, a chunk of bread and a pickled cucumber. He graciously offered some to the two middle-aged men who sat opposite them but they equally graciously declined.

After he had eaten, Misha began to feel sleepy. But just as his eyes were closing a soldier entered the carriage. 'Comrades, please return to the station concourse.'

'That's it,' said Yegor. 'We're not going. The *Vozhd* has decided to stay.'

CHAPTER 22

As Misha and Papa boarded another lorry to return them to the Kremlin, they saw the station concourse was again filling up with ordinary Muscovites. Where they were going and when they would get there, Misha could only wonder.

Moscow seemed just as chaotic on their return journey. 'It would be quicker to walk,' said Yegor.

'Let's walk then,' replied Misha. After all, their cases were going to be loaded on to a separate lorry.

Yegor shook his head. 'Have some sense, Mikhail,' he said. 'It's anarchy out there.'

Misha sat in the back of the lorry, watching the disorder out in the street. Lines from a poem his old literature teacher had shown him at the start of the year came to mind, and he whispered them to himself:

'Things fall apart; the centre cannot hold;
Mere anarchy is loosed upon the world.'

His papa shook his head. 'What's this nonsense?' he said gently.

'Just a poem, Papa,' said Misha. He wasn't going to tell him it was W.B. Yeats. Partly because he knew he wouldn't be interested, and partly because he had a strong idea that the Party would not approve of W.B. Yeats. Certainly his literature teacher had vanished from their lives not long after.

It was five o'clock in the morning by the time Yegor wearily turned the key in the apartment door. 'Go to bed and sleep for as long as you need to,' he said to Misha. 'Don't go to school. Wait here. I will telephone if I need to warn you about anything.'

Misha fell asleep as soon as his head touched his pillow. He slept through another air-raid warning, another parade of lorries coming and going and a torrential hailstorm. He woke to the sound of the Spasskaya Tower clock striking eleven. With a sinking feeling, he remembered he was back in his apartment – barely sixteen hours before he had thought he would never see it again. He was overwhelmed with conflicting emotions. All the things he had thought he was about to escape – the constant memory of his mama there in the apartment, the threat of imminent death in an air raid or battle – were now part of his life again. But at the same time he felt slightly exhilarated, strangely excited. He didn't quite know why.

As he prepared a simple breakfast from the scraps they had left behind, he noticed a note from his papa on the table.

> *Misha, Please collect our suitcases from in front of the Armoury Chamber. Expected 11 a.m.*
> *Papa*

That was a good excuse to drop in on the Golovkins. Let Valya know he was back. He washed quickly and hurried to collect the cases before the rain began again. But as he approached the Armoury Building he saw the unmistakable figure of Anatoly Golovkin being dragged away by two burly men in NKVD uniforms.

He was shouting and struggling but what he was saying was drowned by a passing convoy of trucks. By the time they had passed, Anatoly Golovkin had disappeared, although Misha did see a Black Raven driving towards the Borovitskaya Tower. He shuddered. That was what they called the cars the NKVD used when they went about their business.

The suitcases were waiting exactly where Papa said they would be and he quickly found both of theirs and dragged them to the Arsenal apartment. Then he hurried again to the Armoury and the Golovkins' apartment. He knocked on the door but there was no answer. He knocked again, calling softly, 'Valya, it's me.'

He heard the shuffling of footsteps inside and the door opened a crack.

She pulled him inside and burst into tears. 'Misha, what can I do?'

'Let's go and sit down,' he said, feeling helpless.

He held her hand across the table until she had stopped crying. Her cat, Kotya, leaped up and demanded attention.

'They said he'd been an accomplice to Zhiglov. He went mad. I've never seen him so angry. They dragged him off, shouting and screaming, and they were hitting him to try to shut him up, but the more they did that, the more he shouted. Misha, it was horrible . . .'

'And what about you, Valya? Are you OK?'

She nodded, wiping her eyes. 'I wonder if they'll come back for me. You'd think if they had me down in their book, they would have arrested me at the same time. I don't know, Misha.'

Misha had never seen her look so frightened.

'I tried to say something but they just pushed me aside.'

'I wish I could ask my papa to help,' said Misha. 'See if he would talk to the *Vozhd*. But he has just been telling me how people who do that are arrested themselves.'

'I wouldn't ask you to do that, Misha,' she said. Then she added, 'Isn't that what happened to your mama?'

'How do you know that?'

'I'm sorry, Misha. You did know, didn't you?'

'Papa told me the other day. Why did you never tell me? No, forget I said that. I'm sorry, Valya. We're all whisperers, aren't we? We're all too frightened to talk. We all have secrets we don't want to share for fear of setting off some trapdoor that will swallow us in an instant.'

She squeezed his hand. 'I will go to Beria. I will see if we can come to an arrangement. I know it sounds like madness but I can't sit here and do nothing.'

Misha was aghast. 'Valya . . .' He tailed off. What could he say? People did desperate things when they were in desperate situations. If she thought she could persuade Beria to release her father, who was he to judge?

She had calmed down now. 'Misha, it might work. I honestly can't think of anything else I can do.'

Misha returned to his apartment. Papa had been round with some food from the Kremlin kitchens and had left another note telling him not to venture out beyond the Kremlin walls. The events of the last twenty-four hours caught up with him and he went to his room to rest.

He must have slept for several hours because he was roused from a deep slumber by a persistent knocking at the door. It was Valya again. He was startled when he saw her. Beneath her black winter coat she was wearing her red dress and had a matching red ribbon in her hair. She looked more beautiful than ever and he noticed with a shock she was wearing make-up.

Misha expected more tears but she seemed detached. 'I tried,' she said plainly. 'I saw him in the corridor where we've often crossed paths, and I smiled as seductively as I could manage in the circumstances and asked if I could see him alone. He looked me up and down with a cold smile and I could see he was trying to make his mind up. Then he stroked the side of my face. He said, "Dear little Valentina, you're camp dust," and walked off.'

'That was all?' said Misha.

'What am I going to do? Do I wait at the apartment for the NKVD to arrest me? Shall I pack a suitcase? Do I try to escape? Where would I go?'

Misha was amazed at how calm she was being.

'Valya, stay here and have supper, then you can decide what to do . . .'

He looked in the refrigerator and saw that Papa had left some eggs and a litre of milk. He noticed a new tub of margarine rather than butter. The usual Kremlin luxuries were obviously getting harder to find. Still, there was a fresh loaf in the bread bin, so Misha decided to make scrambled eggs. He was good at scrambled eggs.

He heard a stifled sob and turned back to Valya. Her eyes were full of tears. 'I keep thinking about what they are doing to Papa,' she said.

Misha hugged her awkwardly. 'You must have something to eat. That will make you feel better,' he said, realising how stupid it sounded.

Just as he placed the eggs on the plates and was bringing them to the table the hall door flew off its hinges.

Three NKVD men burst into the dining room. 'Valentina Golovkin, you are to come with us immediately.'

Misha stood up and shouted, 'If you knocked, we would have let you in.' He pointed at the door. 'Look what you have –'

One of the men knocked him to the ground, scattering his cooking over the floor. As he lay reeling from a blow to the side of his head, Valya said, 'Why am I being arrested?'

Misha expected them to hit her too, but they just grabbed her arm. 'You are an enemy of the people,' he heard one of them say.

A burly bear of a man yanked Misha up from the floor, as easily as if he were a small bag of shopping. 'And you, Mikhail Petrov, are aiding an enemy of the people.'

They were dragged out of the apartment and hustled down the corridor, leaving the door wide open and hanging half off its hinges.

CHAPTER 23

A Black Raven was waiting for them just outside the entrance, with its engine running. Misha could guess where they were going. It was a short ride, barely a minute or two. But as the car took its predictable route along these familiar streets his heart began to thump hard in his chest.

The car ground to a halt by a little door at the side of the Lubyanka. Several men waiting on the pavement bundled Misha and Valya out of the Black Raven, kicking them through the door with their shiny black boots. One of the NKVD men grabbed Misha by the scruff of his neck and frogmarched him along. The stench of urine, sweat and a pungent chemical detergent made his nose smart. For a second, he and Valya were bumped together.

'Admit to anything, everything,' she whispered hurriedly.

One of the guards hit her around the head. 'No talking.'

Suddenly Misha realised Valya was no longer with him. Was that the last he would see of her – a pale face, eyes darting around in silent terror? He wondered how long it would be before she betrayed him and what kind of crimes they would accuse him of.

Misha was taken to a small damp cell with whitewashed walls. It was cold enough for him to see his breath in front of him. There were two chairs either side of a small metal table. He was made to sit on one of them under the glare of the bare light bulb and his hands were tied behind his back. Then he was left alone.

He waited, flinching at every footstep outside the door. In the distance he could hear the occasional scream. No one came. After an eternity, the door burst open and a tall, stocky man with cruel eyes and thick, slicked-back hair marched into the room.

'Look to the front,' he said. 'Do not move your head to either side. Do not move or speak without being told to.'

Then he sat down and slammed a file down on the desk between them.

'Mikhail Petrov, you are an enemy of the people. You are contaminated by heresy.'

Misha looked at him, too terrified to speak. He noticed the man was wearing black leather gloves, along with the usual green jacket and black boots of the NKVD.

'You can help me and help yourself by confessing everything now. Your girlfriend –' he spat out the words – 'has already told us all about you. She needed no prompting at all.'

He got up and stood behind Misha, who tensed with fear. An almighty blow knocked him sideways and he yelped with pain as his tethered arm was trapped beneath the chair. His interrogator left him there for a minute, saying nothing, then hauled him upright with surprising ease.

'You are a stick of a boy, Mikhail Petrov. You will not survive a beating. Here is what we know about you.' He opened the file and picked up a thin onion-paper sheet, the typewritten text punched so hard it had created little stencil letters throughout the page.

'You and your partners in crimes against the people, Valentina Golovkin, and the traitor Anatoly Golovkin, have vilely conspired to sabotage the Soviet struggle against the Hitlerites by passing on secret information to German spies and saboteurs in Moscow. You have also transmitted messages to enemy bombers, signalling for them to drop their bombs on the Kremlin when Comrade Stalin was in residence. Furthermore, you have committed acts of sabotage in the Stalin Automobile Plant, deliberately wrecking tank-production machinery and placing explosives on the gun-assembly floor. How do you respond to these charges?'

Misha's head was reeling. He had not even been to the Stalin Automobile Plant since the war began and they had switched to tank production. But he also felt an odd sort of pride. Nothing that this man had said to him could have come from Valya. She hadn't betrayed him at all. This was all complete nonsense. He heeded her words. He would admit everything.

'It's all true. I did everything you have accused me of.'

The man looked at him with contempt. Misha almost expected him to say, 'Surely you're not admitting to this crap. It will get you nine grams in the back of the neck without a doubt. Come on. Put up more of a fight, then I can hit you some more.'

Then he came and stood behind him again. Misha flinched, expecting another blow. But instead, he felt his hands being untied.

'Sign at the bottom.'

Misha tried to grip the pen but his hands were shaking and he had to breathe hard.

'Hurry up,' shouted the interrogator.

Misha scribbled in the indicated space, fully aware that he might be signing his own death sentence.

Then the man produced two more blank pages and

told Misha to sign them too. He did so without a second thought.

The man called for two guards and Misha was whisked away. Whenever they heard other people approaching through the maze of corridors, Misha was roughly turned against the wall so he could not see who they were. They went up two flights of stairs to a room where he was photographed and had his fingerprints taken.

Then they took him back down to the basement and placed him in a crowded holding cell. Misha looked fearfully at his fellow prisoners. Some, he could tell by the cut of their clothes, were important people, perhaps factory managers or Party heads in the Moscow districts, but most of them were young men, probably deserters or looters, with a handful of women and a smattering of hardened criminals. They were easy to tell by the tattoos you could see on their faces and hands.

Misha's heart sank at the thought of being locked away for years with them. He was surprised to find himself completely ignored by everyone around him. But that suited him. He didn't want to talk to anyone either.

He found a space by the wall and tried not to think about what would happen when they came for him again.

Throughout the night people were called from the cell. Some of them returned, usually covered with bruises.

One prisoner was thrown back in the cell whimpering in agony, clutching a broken arm. The next few hours passed in a haze of slammed doors, distant screams and echoing footsteps.

CHAPTER 24

Misha had drifted into an uneasy sleep when he was called from the cell. As he emerged, he was grabbed roughly by two NKVD men and dragged down corridors and up stairways to an outer courtyard where he waited with several other prisoners. The smell of the autumn night air hit him like a wave of clear fresh water and he filled his lungs, feeling his senses return from a numb stupor. But it was cold too, and he began to shiver beneath the cloudy sky. What time it was he could only guess. He felt so dislocated from the real world he hadn't even realised it was night again. As they waited, he heard the distant chimes of the Kremlin's Spasskaya Tower clock and counted to ten.

After a couple of minutes, he began to feel braver and let his gaze wander around his fellow prisoners. Valya was there, staring at the floor – the usual protective gesture of any prisoner who expects to be hit at any moment. He was only a metre or two away from her. They could have spoken to each other without even raising their voices. Misha felt a sharp blow at the back of his head.

'Eyes down,' snapped a guard.

They heard the throb of a lorry engine and shouts from the far side of the courtyard wall. There was a hammering at a small steel door and two of the guards hurried to open it. The prisoners were herded through with kicks and punches, like sheep with vicious dogs, and into the enclosed cargo compartment of the lorry. Inside the compartment there were no guards and Misha immediately went to sit by Valya on one of the narrow benches that ran down each side. She looked haunted but, unlike many of his fellow prisoners, he could see no bruises on her face. Maybe they had not treated her as badly as he had feared.

They reached for each other's hands. Her hair ribbon was gone. Maybe they thought she'd try to hang herself with it. She squeezed his hand tight and was about to speak when two of the burlier guards leaped into the back of the lorry. Just before the doors were slammed shut a small light in the roof came on. The guards stood with two submachine guns pointing at the prisoners.

'No talking, no moving,' said one.

The journey was over in less than a minute. As they emerged from the lorry, Misha looked up to see a building he recognised: Moscow City Central Court. Kicks and punches accompanied them to a holding room. Misha stood by Valya but instinct told them not to let the guards know they knew each other.

The captives were counted off in tens and taken up a narrow staircase to a wood-panelled court room, where they were crammed into the prisoners' dock.

The court had clearly been very busy. Three haggard but stern middle-aged men wearing black gowns were sitting directly opposite them. The man in the centre stood and announced that they were cowards, saboteurs and traitors to the motherland and in accordance with paragraph 58 of the Soviet Criminal Code they were all to be sentenced to the highest measure of punishment: execution by shooting, with all property belonging to them to be confiscated. Sentence was to be carried out immediately with no right of appeal.

One of the women in the dock called out in an anguished, angry voice, 'We have a right, as citizens, to a fair –' but she got no further before she was knocked to the ground by a guard.

Misha, standing next to Valya, felt her visibly wilt when sentence was passed. As they were herded away, she managed to whisper, 'I thought we would be sent to the camps.'

A similar lorry awaited them, and they emerged into the night as the sound of air-raid sirens started to wail across the city. Hurriedly herded into the cargo compartment, they sat in darkness as soon as the door was closed. With no guard present, everyone began to talk. 'Where will they take us?' 'I have not said goodbye to my family.'

Valya said, 'Misha, I'm sorry I got you into this terrible mess. I should never have come to your apartment.'

He couldn't feel angry. 'They would have come for me anyway,' he said. He was surprised at how calm he felt. It was all too unreal. The lorry rocked slightly and the engine started. Only then was Misha seized by a creeping terror. This was going to be their final journey. Would they take them to the outskirts of the city and kill them there? Or would they shoot them back at the Lubyanka?

The two of them sat in silence, holding hands again, as the other passengers raged at their fate. Everyone, it seemed, was talking but no one was listening. He could feel Valya breathing deeply, and guessed she was trying to hold back her tears.

'Let's be brave for each other,' she said.

In the distance a string of explosions rang out and

everyone stayed silent. 'Come on, come and blow us all to bits,' shouted one angry voice in the darkness. 'Finish us off in an instant. Put us out of our torment.'

The truck stopped barely more than a minute away from the courthouse. Misha thought they must be back at the Lubyanka but he didn't recognise the building when they were hustled out of the van. Despite their anger and despair as their final journey began, the other prisoners now seemed infected with a defensive herd instinct. Look down, don't catch anyone's eye. Do exactly what you're told and you will make your last moments easier.

Misha observed the whole scene as if it were happening to someone else. Blood was pounding so hard in his ears he could hear nothing more than the muffled thud of his own heartbeat. When people spoke, he could see their lips moving, but his mind wasn't registering their words; it was all a distant babble.

They passed through an entrance arch with ornate white plasterwork and a heavy wooden gate which led directly through to a large interior courtyard. Here several bonfires were blazing away in strict contravention of air-raid regulations. Despite his overwhelming fear Misha recognised the smell in all its different components. There was burning paper, burning cardboard, a slight whiff of kerosene.

In the distance, bombs were still falling. But the explosions seemed to be coming from over to the east, where most of the factories were.

A small group of NKVD guards were standing by the far wall of the courtyard, the light from the bonfires casting their stark, flickering shadows against a plain brick wall. Nearby was a large goods trolley, the sort you would see at the railway station. Among them one man stood out by nature of his physical presence; he was neither short nor tall but his stocky, muscular build gave the impression of immense strength. He wore the same uniform as the others, but also a green leather apron and thick black gloves. It was the sort of protective clothing a slaughterman might wear in an abattoir. He pulled hard on a cigarette as he listened to another man speak and blew out a great plume of smoke. Then he laughed and the other men around him laughed too. He glanced over to the crowd that was being assembled at the other end of the courtyard. Misha looked away. He had seen the face of his executioner.

NKVD guards surrounded them, rifle bayonets glinting in the firelight. Misha thought a bullet would be a better way to die than a bayonet. It hadn't occurred to him that they would kill him in any other way. A bullet was quick. In the films, when people were shot, they

231

dropped to the ground, lifeless in an instant. In a film he had never seen anyone being killed with a bayonet. He could imagine that was infinitely more agonising and prolonged.

Misha realised Valya was still holding his hand and he glanced over to her face, half lit by the flames. She still looked beautiful to him in that moment. Tear tracks glistened on her cheeks in the light of the fires. He thought with choking sadness of New Year's Eve bonfires and fireworks. He wondered if his papa would ever hear about what had happened to him.

The man in the apron barked over to the other side of the courtyard. 'Right, let's get going. One at a time. This shouldn't take long.'

Two guards grabbed a man at the front of the huddled group and dragged him over to the wall. They held him tight and he struggled with every step. The executioner walked towards him and Misha could see the condemned man wilt as he approached. Unable to tear his eyes away, Misha saw the executioner lean forward and whisper in the man's ear. Misha could bear to look no longer.

A shot rang out and Valya squeezed his hand harder. Other prisoners cried out in alarm and despair. The guards around them pointed their bayonets menacingly close.

'Silence,' said one of the soldiers. 'I will kill the next prisoner to make a sound.'

One at a time, the group were dragged away to their fate. Some of them cried out to Jesus or Stalin just before they were shot; others died without a sound. When he could bear to steal a glance over to the execution spot, Misha saw they were stacking the lifeless bodies in a neat pile on the trolley. His legs began to shake violently and he wondered how much longer he could stand without collapsing. His head began to swim and his legs lost their strength. He couldn't help himself and fell to the ground. As he lay there, he became dimly aware of someone shouting, 'All of you, down. Sit on the ground.' Valya put her hand around his shoulder to support him and he held her hard, surprised at the warmth of her body on this cold autumn night.

The group of prisoners was dwindling. All at once Misha felt a boot nudging him. 'You,' said a harsh voice.

'I love you,' he whispered to Valya, and she kissed him fleetingly on the side of the head as she gave him a final desperate hug.

'Let him go, comrade,' said one of the soldiers. He didn't have the heart to hit her.

Another guard grabbed him roughly by the arm and pulled him to his feet.

The pattern was the same. Two guards held him tightly on each side. Misha's feet dragged behind him, scuffing the grass on the lawn, and then the gravel that formed a wide path around the square sides of the courtyard.

Misha expected his life to flash before him, but all he could sense was the flickering shadows of the fires, the acrid smell of burning, and the sparks and embers that floated in the air around them. Wispy streams of hot breath escaped from his mouth into the cold autumn sky. He looked up and caught a final glimpse of the moon and the stars – diamond points of light and a luminous creamy orb. The night sky had never looked more beautiful.

The man in the apron approached him. 'Kneel to face the wall, comrade. This will be very brief.' Even in his fear, Misha was struck by the calmness in his voice. He had spoken to him so matter-of-factly. Like a dentist about to carry out an unpleasant procedure. He kneeled close to the wall, the gravel sharp on his knees. He felt every breath, sensed every heartbeat, wondering which would be his last. He flinched as the cold barrel of the gun touched the back of his neck and steeled himself to stay still, so the man would not have to shoot him twice.

There was a click, followed by cursing, and the executioner called for another weapon. Misha let out an anguished sob. He was still there. His agony was not yet over. 'Hurry, comrade, I cannot bear to kneel much longer,' he said.

A strange whistling filled his ears, getting louder by the second. He breathed again, wondering why the shot had still not been fired, then a shattering explosion enveloped him like a great wave.

That was it. He was dead. But he was still thinking. He could hear Valya's voice. She was pleading, harsh, desperate. 'Misha, run. Run like hell.'

There was smoke, brick dust, debris everywhere. A brace of bombs had blown a hole in the wall and left the building devastated.

Misha and Valya fled, expecting a bullet in the back at any moment. Misha sensed others fleeing with them. One or two shots flew past them, but there were urgent cries too, inside the courtyard. The guards who had survived had other things to worry about.

Misha and Valya ran until they could run no more and stopped to catch their breath as a nearby clock struck the three-quarter hour. The chimes faded into the night as cold wind howled down the narrow street. Both of them were wearing only the flimsy clothes they had been arrested in.

'Misha, what are we going to do?'

'We can't go home . . .'

Misha choked up when he said that. They were barely ten minutes away from their cosy apartments. Both of them knew, without a shadow of doubt, that they would never see those familiar rooms again. There was a long silence as the towering awfulness of their predicament sank in.

They sheltered in the doorway of an abandoned shop. Valya was the first to speak. 'We've got no money, we're going to freeze to death before the dawn, and if we show our faces back home we'll be shot.' She sounded quite matter-of-fact about it. Then she laughed a cold, graveyard laugh. 'We might as well jump into the Moskva and get it over with.'

Misha shivered at the thought. 'There must be somewhere we can go to, Valya?' Misha was trying to be brave. 'Who can we trust?'

'Could we go to Nikolay?' she said. 'What are his parents like?'

'They're nice people but they're very staunch Party members,' he replied. 'I don't think we can trust them.'

'We have to think quickly,' she said. 'The all-clear will sound soon and when it starts to get light there will be more people about. We must look suspicious like this.'

'We could try my Aunt Mila, but she's over in the

Sparrow Hills. And there's Grandma Olya, she's barely ten minutes away.'

'They're the first people the NKVD would go to, to look for you,' Valya said. 'And if they found us with either of them they would be punished too. Anyway, your Aunt Mila's too far away. We'd be spotted by Militia or die of exposure before we got halfway there.'

Then Misha remembered something. 'What about that woman you helped, on the day the war broke out? Do you remember where she lived?'

'Misha, that's it.' She hugged him. 'That's a brilliant idea. We must go at once. I can't remember the way exactly. And I can't quite remember her name either.'

Misha shook his head. 'Me neither. We'll just have to try to find our way as best we can.'

They hurried through the dark streets. 'It's so difficult to recognise where we are in this blackout,' said Valya. But they both knew this was their best chance. Their only chance. If they could find the old lady before dawn, then maybe she would be able to help them.

'She had a place overlooking a big square,' said Valya, as she panted for breath.

'It was one of those great old apartment buildings

from before the Revolution. She lived on the top floor –
a big apartment, not a *kommunalka*.'

'Hush a second,' said Valya, and held up her hand.
'There's someone coming.'

There were footsteps, two people at least. 'It's probably
a Militia patrol. Quickly, we have to hide.'

They dived behind some shrubbery in the alcove of a
small building. The footsteps came closer. Misha tried to
control his breathing. He could not bear to look and
closed his eyes. He felt dizzy with fear. It was as if he were
standing on the parapet of a very high building. Then
they heard the rattling of a key in a lock. A door opened
and shut, and all was quiet again.

'It's round here somewhere, I'm sure of it,' said Valya.
She peered round a corner and immediately froze. 'Oh
no! Just up the street. Two Militia men.'

'That's just what we need.'

'And they're both carrying submachine guns.'

'Are they coming this way?'

She looked terrified and put a finger to her lips to
shush him.

They could hear voices close by now. Coarse, ugly voices.

'Something going on up ahead.'

'Put your torch on.'

Valya grabbed Misha, turned his back to the wall, and

began to kiss him hard, placing his hand on the small of her back.

Misha was so astonished he froze. She stopped for a moment and hissed, 'Rub your hands up and down my back. Quickly!'

He did as he was instructed. Even in his blind panic, he still noticed how warm she was despite the freezing cold night and how slender the curve of her back.

The torch flashed its light into the shrubbery.

They heard coarse laughter. 'You dirty bastards,' one of the men said. They laughed again and walked away.

Misha continued to kiss her, but Valya immediately broke away and whispered, 'Sorry, Misha, I couldn't think of anything else to do.'

They waited for the footsteps to recede, still holding each other tight. Misha felt her warmth and wondered if he would ever kiss her again.

'Come on,' she said. 'We must be near . . .'

They darted between the shadows, peering into the gloom at the names of side streets.

'It's just round here, I'm sure of it,' Valya said.

They came out into a big tree-lined square. 'Strastnoy Boulevard – this is it. I remember now.'

Most of the buildings here were pre-Revolution and it was difficult remembering which one they had gone to.

239

Misha spotted a distinctive doorway. 'Look, it's here. There's the door, with the great stone archway.'

They looked up. The building was eight storeys high with a short flight of stairs leading to the main entrance. Valya tried the door. It was locked.

'What do we do?' said Misha.

'Wait for someone to come out . . . and then nip in. Sometimes these doors catch on the lock if you don't close them properly.'

'It might work.'

The all-clear siren sounded. That was usually the signal for the streets to fill with people as they flooded out of the air-raid shelters, but not any more. Recently one of the public shelters had been bombed. Hundreds of people had been killed, so now many Muscovites had decided it was just as safe staying in their own apartments. And your home was less likely to be looted that way too.

They hid in the shadows of the apartment stairway shivering with the autumn cold. After a few minutes that felt like an eternity, they heard the door open and a man dashed out and hurried up the street. As soon as he was a safe distance away, they vaulted up the stairs. Valya pressed against the door. Much to their relief it creaked open.

There was a light on in the hallway – a dim bulb

– and they could see the little concierge's kiosk. There was a light on there too. Neither of them dared to speak. They approached the staircase gingerly, expecting to be challenged at any moment. Valya looked at Misha and shrugged. They kept walking up the stairs as quietly as possible.

Halfway up the first flight of stairs Misha looked back at the concierge's kiosk. He could see the top of a bald head. Whoever was in there was flat out, resting on the desk. There was a small bottle of vodka next to him, lying on its side with the cork out.

It took several minutes to quietly climb the creaking stairs and reach the top of the building. Five solid wooden doors faced them in the gloom. They peered anxiously at each door, looking for a name plate they recognised.

ANTONINA OVECHKIN

That was her, they were sure of it.

'She asked you to call her Baba Nina, do you remember?'

They could see a light under the door.

Valya knocked gently. The last thing she wanted was other people coming out to see who was there at that time of night. They listened hard, straining to hear a sound.

CHAPTER 25

There was no answer. 'Maybe she likes to sleep with the light on?' said Misha.

They knocked again, a little louder.

Misha leaned down and put a finger in the letterbox.

Valya pulled him away. 'You'll frighten her.'

There was a movement inside. They heard coughing, then a shuffling of feet. A cat let out an inquisitive miaow.

They stood back, so she could see them through the spyhole in the door.

Antonina Ovechkin opened the door swiftly. Misha noticed there was no sound at all as it swung open. She was someone who knew the value of not having a creaking door.

'I know you two,' she said quietly, rubbing the sleep from her eyes. 'Tell me where I have met you.'

They were both surprised at her attitude. They thought she would be indignant or at least want to know what they thought they were doing, coming to see her at this hour of the day.

But Antonina Ovechkin did not seem remotely flustered or surprised. She beckoned them in.

'Come on then, *devotchka*,' she said to Valya, taking her hand. 'Where have I seen you before?'

'We met you in Gorky Street, after Molotov's speech, when war broke out,' said Valya.

'I remember. You both came here for coffee.' She turned to Misha and took his hand. 'You helped me out, didn't you?'

A silence fell between them, broken only by Antonina Ovechkin's coughing. Then she said, 'You don't need to tell me you are in trouble. Coming here without so much as a jacket or coat. I shall make you tea and you can tell me all about it. When did you last eat?'

'We've been arrested. We managed to escape in the bombing.'

'Well, you have been both very unfortunate and fortunate then. But I shall help you. When I last saw you, I thought, *There are two young people who are going to get into trouble.* And sadly, I was right.'

She beckoned for them to sit on the couch in her living room and left them. Valya could barely keep the grin from her face. 'I can't believe we got here safely,' she whispered to Misha.

They could hear Baba Nina bustling around in her small kitchen and she returned with a tray crammed with two cups of tea, with black bread and butter and jam. It was delicious. Misha realised at once that Baba Nina had some very useful contacts. It was hard enough to get butter in the Kremlin at the moment, and here she was handing it out to strangers.

Misha realised how hungry he was as his stomach gurgled loudly when the food was placed in front of him. As they ate, she told them what she was going to do.

'I have to make a phone call and a friend of mine will come to see you.'

Valya and Misha looked at each other.

'Don't look so startled. He will help you. You'll need papers, false identities, travel permits.'

'Why are you helping us?' asked Valya. She tried to keep the suspicion from her voice.

Baba Nina gave a sweet little smile, and dabbed the corner of her mouth with a handkerchief.

'*Devotchka*, I am eighty-two, I am ill with something nasty, and I am not long for this world. I have ceased to care whether the NKVD knock on my door or not. I don't even care if they beat me up – that will finish me

244

off, and that would be better than taking six months to die from this illness. But I do care about what happens to you and people like you. You are the future of our country. When my husband was taken by the NKVD, along with great men like our General Tukhachevsky, I knew that we were being dragged to hell by beggars on horseback. And we were to blame for it. We had supported Lenin and Stalin in all their cruelties. I was there at the All Union Communist Party Congress where we let Stalin take the reins. We thought we were building a new world and anything was justifiable. Well, we've made a terrible mess of it. I want to make sure I do some good things before I die.'

It was a convincing speech.

'What can we do?' said Valya. 'We have been sentenced to death as enemies of the people. I can't even remember the ridiculous crimes I confessed to.'

Baba Nina put a hand on hers and smiled. 'You must go east, to one of the new towns where they are rebuilding the Moscow factories. You will need new names but that is simple.'

'Have either of you been to Kiev?'

Misha nodded. He had been to visit his brother a few times in the summer holidays.

'Good. Kiev is in German hands now and no one

will be able to check your records. There are few enough records anyway as most were destroyed in the Civil War.' She winked. 'A lot of people come from Kiev. Especially people like you. And I'm sure the Germans will destroy the civic records again when they leave.'

'Do you think we'll ever drive them out?' asked Misha.

'My dear, of course we will,' said Nina. 'Are you a student of history?'

Misha nodded. Valya shook her head. 'She's a scientist,' said Misha.

Baba Nina snorted. 'Scientists. They know how everything works! Everyone should learn from history. Hitler is no historian either or, if he is, he is a very stupid one.' She laughed. 'Look at Napoleon. Do you know the Nazis invaded on almost the very same day he did in 1812. Not a very good omen, is it? The same thing will happen to the Germans. I know because we're Russians. And we don't tolerate invaders.

'Here, I'll tell you a story. My brother worked for three years overseeing the construction of the Kharkov Tractor Factory. They raised it up from a muddy field. In fifteen months they built the steelworks, the machinery, then the tractors. Thousands of them. All this from peasant workers who had only known a horse and cart before the

Revolution. My brother worked shoulder to shoulder with them. When they were behind schedule, they had "storm nights" where they worked till dawn and the factory brass band played to help them along. The Nazis haven't got a chance against people like that. We'll win all right, but a lot of blood will be shed.' She stood up. 'Now I must make a phone call.'

She went out and closed the door. They heard her muffled voice for a moment.

'Do you think we can trust her?' asked Valya.

Misha shrugged. 'Why would we not?'

Valya shook her head slowly. 'We have been around the NKVD for long enough to know they have all sorts of tricks and all sorts of agents.'

Misha nodded and said, 'What else can we do?'

Baba Nina returned. 'I have good news. My friend will be arriving in an hour or so. You can rest if you like. You both look very tired. If you want to wash, I will boil a kettle.'

They needed no further prompting. Misha and Valya both fell asleep immediately, resting on each other's shoulders on Baba Nina's plush sofa. She looked at them both with an indulgent smile, covered them with a blanket and switched off the light.

Misha woke with a start as Valya slept on beside him.

There were voices in the hall. The door opened and he blinked as light flooded into the living room. There in the doorway stood a tall figure in the unmistakable uniform of the NKVD.

CHAPTER 26

Baba Nina seemed unperturbed. She bumbled in behind him. 'This is my friend, Vladimir. I think you can call him that too, is that all right, Vladimir?'

The man smiled and removed his hat, revealing the most brutal cropped haircut. He spoke in a low, deep voice. 'You, young fellow, wake your friend.'

Valya then woke with a start and she too recoiled at the sight of the NKVD man.

They both sat there wondering what was to come next.

'It's fairly simple, what we're going to do,' said Baba Nina. She reminded Misha of a doctor explaining an forthcoming operation to a patient. Maybe she had been a doctor before she retired?

'You will both need passes and travel documents,' said the man. 'I think we shall send you to Lysva – it's a new town not far from Perm. That's far enough away for you to make a fresh start. You both need to make up a new name for yourself. Tell me one that's going to be easy to remember, then I will do the rest.'

They both looked completely blank.

Nina patted Misha on the hand. 'Vladimir speaks good sense. They've just moved a tank factory there and the whole town is full of people who have been displaced by all this terrible business. You will be able to travel there by train in a couple of days, maybe more, and you will be able to find work at the factory.'

She looked at Valya. 'With you, you can work there too, or teach perhaps.'

Misha said, 'I teach a lot already. I could do that too.'

She shook her head. Vladimir explained. 'Boys your age are already volunteering for the partisans. It's a death sentence, sending boys that young into such a brutal war. They won't allow you to teach but we can get you a work permit for the tank factory. Now, quickly, I need some names.'

Valya whispered impatiently. 'Misha, we must do whatever these good people say. We can't quibble about what we're going to do.'

They racked their brains for names.

'Alexander Markov,' Misha said.

'Katerina Markov. We can be brother and sister. That would be sensible, wouldn't it?'

Vladimir nodded. 'As you wish.' Then he picked up his bag and went to the door. Misha and Valya could not hear what he said to Baba Nina but he bent down to kiss her tenderly on the cheek and Valya whispered, 'Do you think he's her son?'

In that instant, Misha had an extraordinary idea. 'Comrade Vladimir, I have a request. Please can I ask you and if it is impossible I will understand. My mother was arrested last year and I know she has been sent to Noya-brsk. It's beyond the Ural Mountains. I understand there is an aeroplane instruments factory being rebuilt there. If there is any possibility of sending us to Noyabrsk, I would be very grateful.'

Vladimir wrote down the location and said he would see what he could do.

When the door clicked shut, Nina came back to talk. 'You must sleep. As long as you like. Here. I have a room for guests.' She opened a door and indicated to a double bed.

Misha fell asleep immediately. When he woke, he did not realise exactly where he was and half expected to be in a cell at the Lubyanka. But the room felt much warmer than that and he opened his eyes to see Valya a foot away from him. There were the salt traces of tears around her eyes, and he felt such tenderness for her. She was his sister now, he remembered. He looked at the angle of the sun through a gap in the thick curtains and guessed it was already mid-afternoon.

Baba Nina prepared him a little breakfast. 'She is not your girlfriend, is she?' Misha felt himself reddening and shook his head. 'I thought not.'

When Valya woke soon after, the three of them sat at the kitchen table and Nina said, 'Vladimir will be back tonight or perhaps tomorrow evening and then you must be prepared to go as soon as he says.'

CHAPTER 27

Yegor Petrov sat in the ruins of his life. This apartment which had promised so much had become his tomb. He had spent his entire Rest Day alone and now it was late in the evening. The solitude was killing him. Here, Anna used to walk through the door loaded with provisions, or greet him with a kiss when he returned after a long day working with the *Vozhd*. His three children had played board games on the floor of their spacious living room. Now there was no one. He thought again of asking his mother if she would like to move in with him. But he knew how much she liked to live on her own. He even began to realise, with some surprise, that he would welcome a visit from Aunt Mila.

The grandfather clock ticked ominously in the corner. Outside, snow slid off the roof, muffling the sound of feet crunching through the square below. But when the snow settled Yegor became aware of the measured step of a squad of soldiers. They were coming closer. Then he heard footsteps on the stairs. He was sure they were coming for him and when he heard an insistent knocking at the door he knew he was right.

So this is it. He took one last look around his home and tried to keep down the racking sob that welled up in his throat. He opened the door carefully. He had fixed it himself and had done a less than perfect job. There was an NKVD colonel with three of his men. 'Comrade Petrov, the *Vozhd* demands to see you.'

Yegor was taken aback. He thought he was going straight to the Lubyanka in a Black Raven. He wondered if he was going to get a proper police car or one of the green ones with *Bread* written incongruously on the side.

'What should I bring?' he blurted out.

The Colonel ignored his question. 'Come,' he demanded.

Stalin's office in the Little Corner was a minute or two's walk away. Now they were there in the ante-room, dense with cigarette smoke. It was all so familiar, and it was often Yegor who showed the anxious visitor into the presence of the *Vozhd* here.

Stalin did not keep him waiting. He opened the door himself and ushered him in.

'Yegor, I have heard your boy Mikhail has disappeared, along with the girl, Golovkin's daughter.'

'Comrade Stalin, I cannot tell you how full of shame I am.'

Stalin poured Yegor a shot of vodka from his decanter and offered him a cigarette. Despite his anguish, and fear, Yegor noticed they were Chesterfields rather than his usual Belomor brand. The *Vozhd* had obviously been visited by some high-ranking Americans. He remembered scheduling the meeting. They were here to discuss arms shipments.

Yegor took a cigarette and failed to light it with his shaking hand. Stalin took his lighter and held it steady for him. The *Vozhd* had been drinking again. Yegor could smell it in his sweat and hear it in the slight slur in his voice.

'You and I have been comrades for twenty years, Yegor. I know the shame you feel when children disgrace you. When Yakov was captured alive, I had to arrest his wife and children because I could not be seen to spare my own family when I insisted on such harsh measures for the rest of our fighting men and women. But this is not a battlefront disgrace. This is a wilful child and we have all suffered wilful children. I want you to stay in your job, you are too useful to me, and I want you to stop worrying about the NKVD. I know you had nothing to do with Mikhail's behaviour.'

He stopped and filled his vodka glass. After a few moments of reflection, he said, 'I also know the shock and shame of losing a wife. Don't worry about that either. When things settle down here, we will find you a new one.' There was a long pause. Yegor wondered if this was his cue to go.

The *Vozhd* started speaking again. 'Now, go back to your quarters. Rest. And be ready for work tomorrow morning. We have a mountain to climb. I hear from sources in Tokyo that the Japanese will not be attacking our eastern territories. The Nazis may have a formidable army, but they have weak allies who do not act alongside them. This at least we can do with our British friends. And, if we are lucky, the Americans, if they are drawn into the war, which I suspect they will be. So now they are no longer needed against the Japanese we can bring up all our Far Eastern divisions to repulse the Hitlerites. Tens of thousands of fresh men, Yegor, and hard too. They are used to fighting in snow. We were right to stay in Moscow. The Nazi advance is slowing. They are not prepared for our winter.'

When the *Vozhd* stopped talking, Yegor Petrov rose to leave.

Stalin said, 'You must forget about Mikhail. Who knows what will happen to him? Who knows where he is?' He stopped and sighed. 'Svetlana liked him very much, you know. But he is gone, just as surely as Yakov has gone. We both know the grief of losing a child and we both know the grief of losing a wife. But you must not concern yourself with your own future.'

'Thank you, Iosif Vissarionovich,' said Yegor, and the two men kissed each other on the cheek, like the old comrades they were.

Yegor Petrov returned to his apartment and poured a large glass of vodka. He was shaking so much he kept spilling it. Only when he had knocked it back in one gulp did the trembling lessen.

He wondered if he could impose on Anatoly Golovkin at this late hour, then remembered with a sudden dread that he too had been taken. He tried to console himself with what he had left. His wife was still alive. That much he hoped was true. Perhaps they would be reunited one day. He remembered with revulsion Comrade Stalin's offer to find him a new wife.

His daughter, Elena, was out there somewhere. She had managed to escape from the Nazis, at least. Who knew what had happened to Viktor? Yegor had seen the casualty figures at work. Maybe two million men and women had disappeared in the first few weeks of the war, almost certainly dead. And he knew their relatives would never know what had happened to them. Perhaps Viktor would turn up one day, out of the blue, with a chest full of medals. Maybe some of the partisans would survive the war. Yegor knew it was equally likely he would die and be buried in an unmarked grave.

And Misha, with his foolish infatuation that had probably cost him his life . . . Dear Misha. He had had such great hopes for him . . . Yegor was certain he would never see him again. He drank down another full glass of vodka and wondered bitterly how a good man like him could deserve such ill fortune.

CHAPTER 28

Vladimir did not return to Antonina Ovechkin's apartment that evening or the next. Baba Nina did not seem overly concerned. 'It is quite normal,' she said, but for Misha and Valya it was agony.

'You must put this time to good use,' said Nina. 'From now on I will only call you by your new names, and that is how you shall address each other. Alexander and Katerina. Sasha and Katya. You must create a believable past life in Kiev. Who were your parents? What did they do? Just have one. Your father left when you were tiny. Are they still alive? No. Your mother died in the fighting. Killed by bombs . . . Keep it as simple as possible.'

'I know Kiev a bit,' said Misha. 'My brother lives there.'

'Papa's family came from there,' said Valya. 'I've been a few times too.'

'Good,' said Nina. 'Write down your story in as much detail as you can. No one will question you on the way, they'll be too busy, but when you get there you'll have busybodies asking questions and you must be ready for them.'

They studied hard, constantly taking it in turns to ask the other their life story. Details of old schoolmates were easy enough. They could use exactly the same friends. They made up an imaginary father and mother, picking their favourite bits from each real parent. That was the most difficult thing to do. Each of them came close to tears.

'We've no time to be sad . . . Sasha,' said Valya, who was finding it difficult to remember to use their new names.

Nina had them go through her collection of spare clothes to find the warmest coats they could. There was a great pile of odds and ends in a large cupboard in the hall. Misha wondered how many other people she had helped. She took the clothes they had arrived in and washed them and ensured they each had their bag packed and ready. 'You must be ready to go at a moment's notice.'

Night fell for the third evening and they retired to bed. 'He will be here tomorrow, I am sure of it,' said Baba Nina.

Misha had discovered Valya was a restless sleeper. She snored like a trooper and often spoke in her sleep. She dreamed often of her papa, calling out for him as he was taken away. Sometimes she woke distraught and they hugged tenderly, like frightened children. Near the dawn, when she saw that he was awake too, she said, 'You know how some of the old people are so bitter and a bit haunted? You feel they are carrying secrets – something terrible that happened to them, or something they did that will spill out one day and that will be it – the early morning knock on the door . . . I think about what else we'll have to live through in this war, and I wonder what sort of parents we'll become, and whether our grandchildren will be frightened of us.'

Misha thought about this. Before they drifted back to sleep he said, 'But Antonina's not like that. She's still kind and terrible things have happened to her. If we survive, Valya, let's try to be like her.'

The following morning Nina woke them with a knock on the door. 'He's been,' she announced with a proud smile and produced a whole pile of documents and passes, all stamped with the seal of the NKVD. She held them up to the light too, so they could see the watermark in the paper. 'My Vladimir always does a very thorough job.'

There were new identity papers, travel permits stamped with the seal of the People's Commissariat of Defence, a succession of train tickets for a journey starting at 3.00 that afternoon from Kazan Station, ration cards, and an address for the barracks where they would stay when they arrived. They were to assemble at the station at 2.00.

Misha hardly dared to look, but when he did he saw the tickets would take them to Noyabrsk.

'We're both going to the aeroplane instruments factory,' he said with a grin.

'Read through your new lives a final time,' instructed Nina. 'Then give me your notes so I can burn them in the stove.'

As they waited out the rest of the morning, they played with Antonina Ovechkin's cat. 'What about your cat, Katya?' asked Misha. 'Are you worried about her?'

She laughed. 'She will look after herself. Kotya doesn't care who feeds her or makes a fuss of her. If the Germans get here, she will make friends with them too. Maybe that's how we will have to survive for the next few years. Make friends with anyone who will do us favours – but not Germans of course! It's a callous way to look at the world, but maybe that's the only way we'll stay alive.'

Moscow was still in chaos when they stepped away from the safety of Antonina Ovechkin's top-floor apartment. They left her with tearful hugs and knew they would never see her again. The last thing she did was press a bag bulging with bread, cheese and dried meat into Misha's hands.

Out in the street it was snowing hard and everyone was hurrying one way or another. Moscow, on the verge of battle, was in utter chaos. Fortunately the route to Kazan Station was simple enough and easy to make on foot – a succession of boulevards led north-east to the terminus. They argued about whether they should walk together or apart. Misha thought it safer to split up. But Valya said, 'We're supposed to be brother and sister.' They walked together.

Kazan Station was a seething mass of milling people, shouting, whistles, crying babies, wailing children. It was hell.

Their instructions were simple. A train to Nizhny Novgorod and then another out to Noyabrsk. In the street no one had asked to see their papers. Here, in the dense crush, a railway guard briefly checked their travel permits and tickets. Aboard the train to Nizhny Novgorod a harassed Militia man had waded through the densely packed passengers, checking their papers. He spent barely ten seconds on each passenger, before he squeezed along to the next. The train left an hour late and steamed unin-terrupted through frequent towns and villages, factories and dense birch forest. Every hour they travelled, the safer they felt.

They waited a day at Nizhny for their connection and discovered scores of other passengers were also going there to work at the new factory. Misha was extremely grateful to Antonina Ovechkin for her advice. He hoped he and Valya sounded convincing in their new identities.

It was dusk and a beautiful light fell over the West Siberian Plain. They had been travelling three days now from Nizhny, and the view from the window had barely changed, save for the passage of the sun across the sky. Valya was asleep, resting her head on Misha's shoulder. He stared out as the endless landscape rolled past to the steady beat of the wheels on the rails. Aside from a few low bushes which cast deep shadows, it was like being adrift on a great pink sea. It was a beautiful country, never more so than when it was covered in snow. Misha had never been this far east before and had never quite realised how huge his country was. He thought of Napoleon, and he thought of the Hitlerites, and he knew in his heart, with absolute conviction, that anyone who invaded his Russia was inviting their own destruction.

The train took a long curve as it began to head north and the black shadow of the locomotive, its carriages and the long, dancing plume of engine smoke, fell out stark against the ground. They would be there soon, maybe in a day or two. Then, when they were settled, Misha was sure he would find his mother.

His eyes felt heavy and, as he began to drift off, a line from Chekhov's *Three Sisters* came into his head: 'Life isn't finished for us yet! We are going to live!'

GLOSSARY OF SOVIET ERA AND RUSSIAN TERMS

Babushka

Grandmother/Grandma. Often used to mean an old lady. Sometimes shortened to *Baba*.

Bourgeois

Middle-class or, more widely, prosperous. Also used to mean having middle-class taste and values, especially those disapproved of by the Soviet regime.

Dacha
(pron. dasha)

Modest holiday or weekend home in the country. Many Russians owned a *dacha*, usually within easy travelling distance of their home town.

Devotchka

Girl or young woman. Used as a term of endearment, like 'darling'.

Kommunalka

Building converted into small, crudely partitioned living spaces, with shared kitchens and bathrooms – a government remedy to the chronic overcrowding in Moscow during the early Soviet era.

Komsomol

Youth wing of the Communist Party. For 16-year-olds upwards who are candidates for Party membership.

Komsorg

Supervisor of *Komsomol* cadets in a school.

NKVD

People's Commissariat for Internal Affairs – the Soviet secret police.

Partisan

Member of the armed groups who fought against the German occupying forces. A particular feature of the war on the Eastern Front.

Politburo	Committee of top ministers in Stalin's government.
Pravda	Soviet era newspaper, written and produced by the regime. *Pravda* means 'truth'.
Proletarian	Member of the working class, such as a factory worker or a labourer.
Rasputitsa	Season of rain and mud that arrives in spring and autumn.
Ulitsa	Street.
Vozhd (pron. Vajd)	Boss. Stalin's staff called him this.

A NOTE ON NAMES

Russian names are a complex business. The name itself is in three parts: a first name, a patronymic (meaning a name derived from the father's name) and a surname. Also, when the person is female, most Russian surnames take an 'a' at the end, for example Petrov becoming Petrova. For the sake of clarity, I have just given my characters a first name and a surname, and I have not changed surnames to reflect gender.

Russian first names are often shortened by friends and family, as they are in the West. For example, my two main characters, Mikhail and Valentina, call each other 'Misha' and 'Valya'.

In the 1920s and 1930s many children were given newly invented names, based on Soviet leaders or Revolutionary themes, such as Barikada (after the barricades Communist soldiers used to defend themselves during the Revolution), Vladlen (based on Vladimir Ilyich Lenin) or Marklen (based on 'Marxist Leninist'). Lenin and Karl Marx were the two leading political theorists of the new Soviet state.

FACT AND FICTION

Although Misha, Valya and their contemporaries are fictional characters, I have tried to depict the circumstances of their lives as realistically as possible. I have also tried to depict Stalin as he was, and many of the incidents about him in this story are inspired by reported events – the notes from his daughter, Svetlana, the conversations between him and his generals, the occasion where his vodka bottle is filled with water.

The incident at Kazan Station, in October 1941, where Stalin decides the government will stay in Moscow, is also based on eyewitness accounts. Most of the characters that surround the *Vozhd* are real too: Beria, Rokossovsky, Zhukov, Molotov, as is their reported behaviour.

After unsatisfactory experiments with a six day week in the 1930s the Presidium of the Supreme Soviet restored the seven-day week in 1940. As I understand it, the days of the week were given numbers rather than names – Day One, Day Two, etc. – and the seventh day was known as Rest Day. Despite this, most of the population still referred to days of the week by their original pre-Revolutionary names.

I have taken some liberties with the structure and personnel in Stalin's secretarial staff. Yegor Petrov performs some of the duties of Stalin's actual secretary, Alexander Poskrebyshev, although Yegor is an entirely fictional character.

ACKNOWLEDGEMENTS

Thanks as ever to my magnificent editorial team, Ele Fountain and Isabel Ford, who shaped and polished the story with tact and dexterity. My agent, Charlie Viney, offered valuable advice and support. I would also like to thank Simon Tudhope, Jane and Jessica Chisholm, Tom Dickins, Nick de Somogyi and Olga Bakeeva for their help.

Thanks too to Jenny and Josie Dowswell, and Dilys Dowswell, for their support and advice.

And finally . . . Bill Ryan, who I met through the Historical Writers Association, showed extraordinary generosity by lending me many rare books, and a couple of invaluable tourist guides, including one from 1937, which were a great inspiration.

Special thanks are due to Tatyana and Valeri Mescheryakova, who showed me the greatest kindness when I visited Moscow to research this book. The six days I spent in the Russian capital were among the most memorable of my life. Tatyana also told me the story about her great-grandfather, who was signals officer on the Battleship *Potemkin*, and I'm grateful to her for allowing me to incorporate this into the plot.

PICK UP THE NEXT
INCREDIBLE THRILLER FROM
PAUL DOWSWELL . . .

AUSLÄNDER

'DOWSWELL SHOWS US A SIDE OF
NAZI GERMANY RARELY SEEN . . .
A HEART-STOPPING READ'

SUNDAY TELEGRAPH

TURN OVER TO READ CHAPTER 1

CHAPTER 1

Warsaw
August 2, 1941

Piotr Bruck shivered in the cold as he waited with twenty or so other naked boys in the long draughty corridor. He carried his clothes in an untidy bundle and hugged them close to his chest to try to keep warm. The late summer day was overcast and the rain had not let up since daybreak. He could see the goose pimples on the scrawny shoulder of the boy in front. That boy was shivering too, maybe from cold, maybe from fear. Two men in starched white coats sat at a table at the front of the line. They were giving each boy a cursory examination with strange-looking instruments. Some boys were sent to the room at the left of the table. Others were curtly dismissed to the room at the right.

Piotr and the other boys had been ordered to be silent and not look around. He willed his eyes to stay firmly fixed forward. So strong was Piotr's fear, he felt almost detached from his body. Every movement he made seemed unnatural, forced. The only thing keeping him in the here and now was a desperate ache in his bladder. Piotr knew there was no point asking for permission to use the lavatory. When the soldiers had descended on the orphanage to hustle the boys from their beds and into a waiting van, he had asked to go. But he got a sharp cuff round the ear for talking out of turn.

The soldiers had first come to the orphanage two

weeks ago. They had been back several times since. Sometimes they took boys, sometimes girls. Some of the boys in Piotr's overcrowded dormitory had been glad to see them go: 'More food for us, more room too, what's the problem?' said one. Only a few of the children came back. Those willing to tell what had happened had muttered something about being photographed and measured.

Now, just ahead in the corridor, Piotr could see several soldiers in black uniforms. The sort with lightning insignia on the collars. Some had dogs – fierce Alsatians who strained restlessly at their chain leashes. He had seen men like this before. They had come to his village during the fighting. He had seen first-hand what they were capable of.

There was another man watching them. He wore the same lightning insignia as the soldiers, but his was bold and large on the breast pocket of his white coat. He stood close to Piotr, tall and commanding, arms held behind his back, overseeing this mysterious procedure. When he turned around, Piotr noticed he carried a short leather riding whip. The man's dark hair flopped lankly over the top of his head, but it was shaved at the sides, in the German style, a good seven or eight centimetres above the ears.

Observing the boys through black-rimmed spectacles he would nod or shake his head as his eyes passed along the line. Most of the boys, Piotr noticed, were blond like him, although a few had darker hair.

The man had the self-assured air of a doctor, but what he reminded Piotr of most was a farmer, examining his pigs and wondering which would fetch the best price at the village market. He caught Piotr staring and tutted impatiently through tight, thin lips, signalling for him to look to the front with a brisk, semicircular motion of his index finger.

Now Piotr was only three rows from the table, and could hear snippets of the conversation between the two men there. 'Why was this one brought in?' Then louder to the boy before him. 'To the right, quick, before you feel my boot up your arse.'

Piotr edged forward. He could see the room to the right led directly to another corridor and an open door that led outside. No wonder there was such a draught. Beyond was a covered wagon where he glimpsed sullen young faces and guards with bayonets on their rifles. He felt another sharp slap to the back of his head. 'Eyes forward!' yelled a soldier. Piotr thought he was going to wet himself, he was so terrified.

On the table was a large box file. Stencilled on it in bold black letters were the words:

RACE AND SETTLEMENT MAIN OFFICE

Now Piotr was at the front of the queue praying hard not to be sent to the room on the right. One of the men in the starched white coats was looking directly at him. He smiled and turned to his companion who was reaching for a strange device that reminded Piotr of a pair of spindly pincers. There were several of these on the table. They looked like sinister medical instruments, but their purpose was not to extend or hold open human orifices or surgical incisions. These pincers had centimetre measurements indented along their polished steel edges.

'We hardly need to bother,' he said to his companion. 'He looks just like that boy in the *Hitler-Jugend* poster.'

They set the pincers either side of his ears, taking swift measurements of his face. The man indicated he should go to the room on the left with a smile. Piotr scurried in. There, other boys were dressed and waiting. As his fear subsided, he felt foolish standing there naked, clutching his clothes. There were no soldiers here, just two nurses, one stout and maternal, the other young and petite. Piotr blushed crimson. He saw a door marked *Herren* and dashed inside.

The ache in his bladder gone, Piotr felt light-headed with relief. They had not sent him to the room on the right and the covered wagon. He was here with the nurses. There was a table with biscuits, and tumblers and a jug of water. He found a spot over by the window and hurriedly dressed. He had arrived at the orphanage with only the clothes he stood up in and these were a second set they had given him. He sometimes wondered who his grubby pullover had belonged to and hoped its previous owner had grown out of it rather than died.

Piotr looked around at the other boys here with him. He recognised several faces but there was no one here he would call a friend.

Outside in the corridor he heard the scrape of wood on polished floor. The table was being folded away. The selection was over. The last few boys quickly dressed as the older nurse clapped her hands to call everyone to attention.

'Children,' she said in a rasping German accent, stumbling clumsily round the Polish words. 'Very important gentleman here to talk. Who speak German?'

No one came forward.

'Come now,' she smiled. 'Do not be shy.'

Piotr could sense that this woman meant him no harm. He stepped forward, and addressed her in fluent German.

'Well, you are a clever one,' she replied in German, putting a chubby arm around his shoulder. 'Where did you learn to speak like that?'

'My parents, miss,' said Piotr. 'They both speak –' Then he stopped and his voice faltered. 'They both spoke German.'

The nurse hugged him harder as he fought back tears. No one had treated him this kindly at the orphanage.

'Now who are you, mein Junge?' she said. Between sobs he blurted out his name.

'Pull yourself together, young Piotr,' she whispered in German. 'The Doktor is not the most patient fellow.'

The tall, dark-haired man Piotr had seen earlier strolled into the room. He stood close to the nurse and asked her which of the boys spoke German. 'Just give me a moment with this one,' she said. She turned back to Piotr and said gently, 'Now dry those eyes. I want you to tell these children what the Doktor says.'

She pinched his cheek and Piotr stood nervously at the front of the room, waiting for the man to begin talking.

He spoke loudly, in short, clear sentences, allowing Piotr time to translate.

'My name is Doktor Fischer . . . I have something very special to tell you . . . You boys have been chosen as candidates . . . for the honour of being reclaimed by the German National Community . . . You will undergo further examinations . . . to establish your racial value . . .

and whether or not you are worthy of such an honour . . . Some of you will fail and be sent back to your own people.'

He paused, looking them over like a stern school-teacher.

'Those of you who are judged to be *Volksdeutsche* – of German blood – will be taken to the Fatherland . . . and found good German homes and German families.'

Piotr felt a glimmer of excitement, but as the other boys listened their eyes grew wide with shock. The room fell silent. Doktor Fischer turned on his heels and was gone. Then there was uproar – crying and angry shouting. Immediately, the Doktor sprang back into the room and cracked his whip against the door frame. Two soldiers stood behind him.

'How dare you react with such ingratitude. You will assist my staff in this process,' he yelled and the noise subsided instantly. 'And you will not want to be one of those left behind.'

Piotr shouted out these final remarks in Polish. He was too preoccupied trying to translate this stream of words to notice an angry boy walking purposefully towards him. The boy punched him hard on the side of the head and knocked him to the floor. 'Traitor,' he spat, as he was dragged away by a soldier.

SEKTION 20

'A GREAT THRILLER WITH A POIGNANT
HISTORICAL BACKGROUND . . . TERRIFIC'

BOOKSELLER

Alex lives in East Berlin. The Cold War is raging and
he and his family are forbidden to leave. But the longer
he stays, the more danger he is in. Alex is no longer
pretending to be a model East German, and the Stasi
have noticed. They are watching him.

One false move will bring East and West together in a
terrifying stand-off which will change everything for
Alex and his family . . . for ever.